November Grass

A California Legacy Book

Santa Clara University and Heyday Books are pleased to publish the
California Legacy series, vibrant and relevant writings drawn from
California's past and present.

Santa Clara University—founded in 1851 on the site of the eighth of
California's original twenty-one missions—is the oldest institution of
higher learning in the state. A Jesuit institution, it is particularly aware
of its contribution to California's cultural heritage and its responsibility
to preserve and celebrate that heritage.

Heyday Books, founded in 1974, specializes in critically acclaimed
books on California literature, history, natural history, and ethnic studies.

Books in the California Legacy series will appear as anthologies,
single-author collections, reprints of important books, and original
works. Taken together, these volumes will bring readers a new perspective on California's cultural life, a perspective that honors diversity and
finds great pleasure in the eloquence of human expression.

Series Editor: Terry Beers; *Publisher:* Malcolm Margolin.
Advisory Committee: Steven Becker, William Deverell, Peter Facione,
Charles Faulhaben, David Fine, Steven Gilbar, Dana Gioia, Ron
Hanson, Gerald Haslam, Robert Hass, Timothy Hodson, James
Houston, Jeanne Wakatsuki Houston, Maxine Hong Kingston, Frank
LaPena, Ursula K. Le Guin, Jeff Lustig, Tillie Olsen, Ishmael Reed,
Robert Senkewicz, Gary Snyder, Kevin Starr, Richard Walker, Alice
Waters, Jennifer Watts, Al Young.

Thanks to the English Department at Santa Clara University and to
Regis McKenna for their support of the California Legacy series.

November Grass

Judy Van der Veer

foreword by

Ursula K. Le Guin

Santa Clara University ✑ Santa Clara
Heyday Books ✑ Berkeley

Library of Congress Cataloging-in-Publication Data

Van der Veer, Judy.
  November grass / Judy Van der Veer ; introduction by Ursula K.
Le Guin.
      p. cm. -- (A California legacy book)
  ISBN 1-890771-39-2
  1. San Diego County (Calif.)--Fiction. 2. Women ranchers--
Fiction. 3. Young women--Fiction. 4. Ranch life--Fiction. 5.
Cowgirls--Fiction. I. Title. II. Series.
  PS3543.A542 N6 2001
  813'.52--dc21
                                        2001000772

Cover Art: Carolyn Shaw, "Horses near Deer Creek," oil on canvas,
    20"x 30"(1999). Courtesy of The California Heritage Gallery.
Cover and Interior Design: Rebecca LeGates
Printing and Binding: Publishers Press, Salt Lake City, UT

Orders, inquiries, and correspondence should be addressed to:
      Heyday Books
      P. O. Box 9145, Berkeley, CA 94709
      (510) 549-3564, Fax (510) 549-1889
      www.heydaybooks.com

Printed in the United States of America

10 9 8 7 6 5 4 3 2 1

FOREWORD ✑

Ursula K. Le Guin

In the valleys east of San Diego, in a dry year, by late autumn the grass is dry and grey, the pastures are used up. Ranchers may have to take their cattle outside the fences, along the roads, to forage till the rains come and new grass greens the open hills.

That is the season and the setting of this beautiful book, half novel, half meditation. A twenty-three-year-old farm woman watches over her small herd grazing along a roadside where few cars pass, and she thinks about years gone by and years to come, living the timeless days of the shepherd's and the herder's life, a slow and certain rhythm that frees the mind to consider the changes of the earth and the ways of beasts and men. Her heart and mind are clear, her feelings sharp, intense, contained. Everything is seen with the extreme vividness of the dry autumn light of California, when each object is distinct in itself and the line of the hills is achingly pure against the sky.

I bought *November Grass* years ago in a battered secondhand paperback, one of Ballantine's Comstock Editions.

I had never heard of the book or the author and was drawn to it only by the painting of hills on the cover and the descriptive blurb—"A penetrating portrait of California's Great Central Valley." Well, it's not the Great Valley, it's farther south, but it is absolutely California. For those who already love the hills and valleys of California, the poignant accuracy of the landscape and the weather will be a joy; for those whose idea of the West is Malibu and Disneyland, it could be a revelation.

Van der Veer gives us a rural landscape as deeply known and lived in as Willa Cather's Nebraska or Sarah Jewett's Maine. The valley ranches of John Steinbeck's *The Red Pony* and *East of Eden* are natural comparisons, but Van der Veer's picture is truer, I think, to the patient obscurity of the lives and deaths of those who live on and from this austere land. Steinbeck knew his valley, he wrote as a native son, but—like Robinson Jeffers, another great landscapist—he filled up the foreground of his picture with cataclysmically violent human drama. Van der Veer sees the human presence as an element of a larger whole, and perhaps she shows the cruelty of life more truly by showing life as not only cruel. Pain, suffering, grief are intense in her story, but not more intense than tenderness and praise.

At first the book seems not so much a story as a serene autumnal mood piece, so subtly is it told, by indirection and the lightest touches, so gently are we brought to heartbreak. "She had pondered so much about accepting things, now she knew that it wasn't a question of accepting anything. She didn't accept tragedy. Tragedy accepted her."

One of the mysteries of the storyteller's art is that what the writer can say without actually saying it has a power greater than any words. Van der Veer is a master of this magic silence. She tells a love story almost between the lines: it happens before the story begins, and in the pondering mind of the girl herding cows; it comes to grief as indirectly, through a few words spoken by an old man—and it is as stark and haunting as an old ballad.

In a late chapter she describes a beautiful filly, Flaxie. Rearing Flaxie by hand when the mother dies, the girl has of course bonded with her: "She couldn't even think of the colt without feeling all soft with love." The scene seems to be set for the brutal misery of *The Red Pony*. But Van der Veer only says, "No matter what could ever happen to Flaxie the girl couldn't lose her....It was comforting to think that there are some things that neither life nor death can take away." Too easy a comfort, one might say, if one had not read the paragraph that faces the opening chapter of the book: "November Grass is a work of fiction. The only character taken from life is the colt, Flaxie, and Flaxie is dead."

There is no easy comfort in this book. It is earned, hard, true comfort. The book tells us that all we can do is accept; but it's not enough. And it tells us that to accept is not enough; but it's all we can do.

One of the shadows that lies across the bright land of the story is that of war; and again it is sketched with a single line—and the knowledge that the book was published first in 1940. Violence is all outside the story. But the threat of disaster, the sense of the absolute contingency of happiness, of life, is vivid.

The cows, bulls, horses, and goats that populate the book are vivid characters, fellow beings very like human beings in their needs, joys, and mortal fears. To write about animals without sentimentalising or anthropomorphising them, the limits and the depths of this likeness must be both deeply felt and clearly understood. The writer who can write about animals without patronising either them or the reader is very rare. Knowing this, or because they're city folk cut off from the nonhuman world, many critics disdain all writing about animals, dismissing it unread as soppy, childish. But nothing useful or valid can be said about the place of humanity in nature, in the world, if we can't talk about the lives we share the world with. A writer like Van der Veer deserves to be appreciated for her rare, real knowledge and celebrated for her celebration of these other lives. And Van der Veer was indeed what she wrote about: a ranch woman, working on the land and with animals all her life.

There is much charm and dry humor in the animal tales, such as the story of Jesus the goat or the adventures of the Jersey bull Joseph (the strongest male character in the book). But under the laughter, death and pain are always waiting, in the hot, bright sunlight, the cold, black shadows of November.

The central figure is never named; she is "the girl." The first time I read the book I took this for a rather dated affectation of universality, and it bothered me; a simple name is just as universal, without the affectation. But as I went on reading a prose so direct, plain, pure, and strong that it slowed me down to savor it like the taste of honey or a fine liqueur, a completely unaffected language perfectly fitted to its subjects, I began to think that the namelessness of the protagonist implies no pretension to universality, but simply a profound reserve, a genuine wish to be unnamed.

Modesty isn't a trendy virtue at present, and it's always a liability for an artist. Van der Veer published two other adult books, several books for children, and many newspaper pieces in papers of the San Diego area and the *Christian Science Monitor*. Clearly she sought and found publication, was as professional in her writing as in her ranching. But then how could a book of this quality go so generally unknown, and disappear so soon and so absolutely?

A silly question. It happens all the time. The quiet book may always get crowded out by the noisy ones, the subtle book by the crass ones; and the best seller commodity machine was functioning in 1940, though it was not quite as efficient as it is now at institutionalising mediocrity. But I can't help feeling that in this case, the author's personality had something to do with the book's fate. Stronger than the blatant authorial ego we are so familiar with is the reticence of the ranch woman: the distrust of wordy, greedy folk; the pride. This author is soft-spoken and generous, she invites you in, entertains and feeds you well, sends you contented on your way. Only when you're a mile down the road, thinking gratefully of her, do you realise that she never told you her name.

February 2001

Dedicated to Marion Ethel Hamilton

November Grass is a work of fiction.
The only character taken from life is the colt, Flaxie,
and Flaxie is dead.

CHAPTER 1 ⁀

In November the girl began taking the cattle out to graze on roadside grass. All the dry grass was gone from the hill pasture and the last of the corn fodder was fed. Usually the corn fodder lasted until winter rains brought up new pasturage, but this summer the big field was turned for summer fallow; it was an old field and needed rest. The little field raised a good crop of corn but not enough to last until grass time. If the cattle got their fill of roadside forage they wouldn't need much hay, and saving hay was as good as saving money. By the roadside there were patches of Bermuda grass and plenty of tall brown grass; even the oldest cow could get enough to eat.

After the morning milking was done, the girl put a hackamore on Pete and rode him bareback, hazing the cows ahead of her. The old hound, Juno, walked at Pete's heels and Flaxie, the yearling filly, cavorted beside him. Sometimes the colt made sudden sallies, rushing up at the cows and making them trot until their empty udders swished back and forth. She was so beautiful and lively in the crisp morning that the girl took pleasure in watching her.

All the girl had to do was to stay near the cattle so they wouldn't wander too far or break into neighbors' fields. If any of them got in the road she shooed them out of the way when a car came along. But the road was so little traveled that the passing of a car became an event.

Some people thought herding cattle a monotonous job, but the girl enjoyed it. She liked the sound the browsing animals made, breaking off the sun-crisped grasses. It was satisfying to see the lean cows eat their fill.

Once the cattle settled down to grazing she turned Pete loose so he could eat, too. Flaxie the colt stopped her foolishness and grazed earnestly. The girl sat down and the hound went to sleep beside her. Sometimes the old dog dreamed. She whimpered and jerked her legs, thinking she was chasing rabbits over the hills.

The girl could drowse in the warm grass, or read a book if she brought one, or just sit and think. That was what made her occupation so pleasant. Apparently she was doing nothing but being lazy, yet she was tending to the very important job of feeding cattle.

This was the time of year for waiting. It was between the time of harvesting and the time of planting. The wild grass seeds were dormant in the hard earth. The farmers had to wait until rain came before they could plow and plant oats and barley. There was a hard dry crust over the fields where a few months ago corn had been tall and bright.

The corn had been so beautiful! The girl had helped with the irrigating and cultivating and because she worked with it so much it had grown, almost, to have a personality. She remembered how it had been when she went to walk up and down the rows one summer night. The corn was bright with light and deep with shadow, and breathless with growing under the August corn moon. And, soon after, all the stalks were cut and carried away. Now the field must wait a while, then it would receive oat seeds, and in the spring, oats would be cut and, after the cattle had gleaned the field, it would be plowed again and corn planted. Though the season now seemed slow of turning and nothing could be planted and nothing grew in the pastures, it was a good season. It was part of the cycle, though it seemed the stopping time.

The fields were waiting for their turn to be planted, first with grain, then with corn. The hills were waiting for the time of grass and wildflowers, for the time of young rabbits and coyote pups and fawns and grazing cattle again. Leaves dropped from sycamores, cottonwoods and willows, but the live oaks held their leaves, growing only a little more dusty looking as the days went on.

Though the land was very thirsty, so thirsty that even cactus looked as if it wanted rain, and dust was ankle deep in cattle trails, there was actually more surface water in places than in midsummer. Everywhere under the earth water was rising as if unbearably eager to meet water from the sky. You had only to dig a little hole in the sandy riverbed, and there was water. Springs that had been nearly dry in August were reviving now, and where tules were yellowing in the swampy bits of riverbed, you saw that the water had risen. A remarkable thing to be happening after seven rainless months, but it happened every fall. Old folks said that it was because of colder nights, but the girl liked to think it was because water was anxious to be moving, now that it was time for rain. Once the rains really started there would be rushing torrents everywhere, everything would seem moving with excitement. It would be the time of year for hurry, tractors would drone until dark in the fields, horses and men would work themselves weary.

But now there was little work, and that, slow. Other men were doing what her father was doing, spreading manure on waiting fields, and between times hauling dead wood out of the river to burn when cold weather really came.

The only lively creatures this time of year were the turkeys. Their gobbling increased as the days went by. It was a sound you never heard in the spring; it belonged to fall as much as withered leaves and dry fields. It would seem to rise to a crescendo until Thanksgiving, then decrease until after Christmas, not to be heard until October again.

The cows were bred, except the heifer whose first calf stayed home in the corral. The cows and mares were quiet this time of year; in the spring they would rejoice in new calves and colts, then grow restless, longing to be bred again. But now it was their quiet time, and their hungry time, too. They probably had forgotten that grass is sometimes green.

The girl sat and looked around her at the waiting world. It was a yellow and brown world, with sparse touches of green. It was a world bordered by mountains. Their rocky sides turned red at sundown and gray blue at noon. It was all a little too bright, like a girl waiting eagerly for a lover coming. For though middays were hot and drowsy, there was a feeling of expectancy. There was a tenseness in the waiting; the world wasn't so relaxed as the dropping leaves might indicate.

But the girl felt relaxed. Summer had been a time of work, and a time of play, too. Summer had been a time of wonderment, and she must think about that later. Now this was different. This was a time to stop and look at the land before rain changed it. This was a time to look at herself before years changed her.

CHAPTER 2 ~

The road was narrow, little more than a lane. It was a winding road, with a high hill on one side and the dry river on the other. Between the road and the riverbed were fenced fields and pastures, but there were no fences on the hillside, so the cattle could graze a way on the first slopes before the hill grew steep and stony.

Some sycamores and live oaks stood near the road, and big boulders, rolled down the hill a thousand years ago, were cold in the morning and hot at noon. Thickets of wild tobacco and willow and goldenrod grew along the fence. The goldenrod had turned fuzzy and had a pleasant bitter dusty smell. On wild-rose bushes were bright red berries that had been the hearts of pink roses. They would make better Christmas trimmings than holly.

By the river, cottonwood leaves rippled when a wind blew. Some of them were yellow. Willow leaves looked like curled segments of dried oranges, and the falling sycamore leaves were rust color. For all the dryness of the earth the land was a colored land. When the girl climbed the hill and looked across the valley she saw bright leaves and blue mountains, and red and white and black and yellow cattle in the river pastures.

Now the days were all alike, being bitter cold toward morning and breathlessly dry and hot before noon. Then shadows were printed sharply black and cold on the dusty earth. In the morning only the mountain tops were in sunshine. The valley was full of chilly shadows, and brush rabbits and cottontails ran swiftly across the road, as if to warm themselves. Not many birds felt like singing then. Water looked icy in a swampy bit of river beyond the fence; the tules shivered. A few mud hens spoke harshly, but the red-winged blackbirds that had whistled music at sundown seemed only half awake now.

But in a short time sunlight came down the hills and the north side of the valley began to grow warm. The south side was still cold with shadow. Cattle and horses stood hunched up, waiting for the sun to warm them. When the rocks began to grow warm the ground squirrels came out of their burrows. Sometimes the old hound chased one. The squirrel would reach a safe high rock and sit on its haunches and scold, its tail jerking to emphasize its excited remarks.

Woodpeckers pounded on trees, quail called in the brush, canyon wrens sang, and sparrows and smaller birds chirped and whistled. Hummingbirds, no bigger than a man's thumb, whizzed among the wild-tobacco blossoms. They perched on nothing but air, their wings moving so fast they were nearly invisible. They had green backs and red throats; they stabbed long bills into yellow trumpet-shaped blossoms, among blue green leaves.

The road really wasn't a quiet place, after all. It had a life of its own. Tiny paths were pressed in the hillside grass. These trails were used by rabbits and squirrels; they crossed the road on the way to the river. Scrawny clumsy-looking roadrunners seemed always in a hurry. The girl was interested in these birds that were so different from others. They wouldn't fly unless they had to. The road had fresh writings on it every morning. The girl could read them. Elflike bands of quail left delicate tracings that made a chainlike pattern. Possums left little handlike tracks. There were graceful dancey marks from feet and tails of kangaroo rats. Rabbits, squirrels and skunks left their prints. Sometimes coyote dung was in the middle of the road. Coyotes were hungry in the fall when rabbits were grown and hard to catch among the brush and rocks. There were grapes in coyote dung. There were scratches in the dust where the coyote had scuffed with his hind feet like a dog.

Sometimes the girl saw a tarantula sauntering along. It would feel out ahead with its furry front legs before it set them down. The big spiders looked warm and soft in their shining black fur. Indians said you could expect rain when you saw tarantulas walking uphill. So far the girl had seen none climbing.

Bright black stinkbugs walked the road. If anything touched one it stood on its head and thought it was safe. If it was touched again it let out a bitter odor.

There was a whole world of beings close to the earth in the jungle of grass stems. Small things lived, fought, mated and died without ever knowing that giants walked the land. Lives so small that a speckled ladybug on a stem was a monster in comparison. The girl could join that world by lying down in the dry grass and looking through the stems. If she half closed her eyes that world was a colored world, too. Little crystals of color gathered on the trunks of grass.

And under the earth's surface was another world. Sometimes a grass stem would quiver and shake when no breeze was blowing. An inhabitant of the underworld was gnawing at its roots. There beneath the grass were dark corridors and vaulted rooms, and nurseries for the blind young. It was a dangerous world, that world of grass stems and underground passages. Its inhabitants had to be as wary as deer in the hills.

Under fallen sycamore leaves the girl heard a thin screaming. By the time she got hold of a king snake's tail there was silence. She held the twisting snake high and saw a bulge in its throat. Had she a knife, she might have cut it open to see if a small mouse would creep out alive.

But she wasn't sure that she would have cut it open. A snake had to eat. King snakes are considered good snakes; it is said that they kill rattlers. This might be the last snake she would see for a while. They didn't appear in cold weather. Before she tossed it over the fence into the field she regarded the snake for several moments, watching the sun shine on its beautifully patterned skin. It twisted as it sailed through the air—it must have been surprised to find itself flying. It would have been more surprised if it could understand that man considered it a relative of birds. It preyed on its relations, robbing nests of eggs and young. Its relations, in the form of roadrunners, preyed on it.

The girl's sympathies were divided between the eater and the eaten. She felt sorry for rabbits the coyotes caught; at the same time she was glad for the hungry coyotes. She felt sorry for the mouse inside the snake, but she wouldn't have enjoyed cutting the snake open. She was sorry that mountain lions killed deer to eat, but it wasn't so bad as hunters killing them for sport.

The world of brown hills and unflowing rivers was a harsh home for those who dwelt there. Yet each had a defense. The fawns learned to hide, breathlessly still. Rabbits and coyotes could fit into the hills' color scheme. Rabbits could even fight if they had to. Once a man told her that he had seen a mother rabbit stamp a rattlesnake to death with her strong hind legs. The snake was after her babies.

When they were very young the children of hills and riverbed had to learn to hide or run or fight. Kill or be killed. And male and female forever seeking each other to call more lives into being. More things to be the eaters or the eaten.

On the surface the world was beautiful and tranquil, but if you looked beneath the surface beauty you saw terror and pain. It was like seeing a still shining pond and then looking in it, beyond your reflection, and seeing loathsome blood suckers.

It was reassuring to look at the grazing cattle. They destroyed nothing. The November grass they ate was already dead.

CHAPTER 3 ✑

One morning Louie Olson came along her way. The girl felt a trifle uneasy as he climbed out of his car to sit beside her on the grass. It was time Louie was looking for a new wife, and the girl hoped she wasn't being considered as a candidate. Louie's wives always worked too hard. Louie was the gentlest, kindest and most helpless of men; everything he tried to do went wrong so that a woman's love for him was strengthened by pity. His wives had acted as if they enjoyed working themselves to death. He was the kind of man that a woman wants to help and manage.

Someone would marry him soon. He had been growing increasingly forlorn and shabby in the six months since his last wife died. His cow would not get with calf, his sow ate her pigs, his most willing horse died, his hens went into a decline. Even during the dry season weeds grew in his fields. He was looking as if he did not have enough to eat and a woman could see how badly his clothes needed mending. His appearance would make most any female feel energetic. There was so much that wanted doing.

Spilling a goodly portion of tobacco he rolled a cigarette. "How's things going?" he inquired. His questions never seemed to demand an answer. He spoke with such an exaggerated drawl that it seemed as if he had a speech impediment. He was from "back east" somewhere in the Middle West, but the girl had never heard any other Middle Westerner use a drawl like Louie's. Though it took him a long time to say anything, he didn't fumble for words as some slow talkers do, so people listened to him with patience. It always seemed as though he were going to say something very important.

"What do you do, sitting here half of every day? Don't it get wearisome?"

"I sort of like it," the girl told him. "Sometimes I half go to sleep, sometimes I just sit and think, sometimes I read a book."

Louie nodded. "I never mind just sitting somewhere. Seems like there's an awful lot a body can think about. You wouldn't know it to look at me, but I got idees about most everything they is."

He took a satisfying drag on his cigarette before it came apart and spilled hot ashes and tobacco on his jacket.

"Dang it," he said mildly, and let the girl brush off the sparks. "Seems like I never do get a cigarette made right."

"You'll burn yourself up some day," she told him. "I hope you never smoke in bed."

"Ella used to try to cure me of smokin' at all. Said it would be safer for me to chaw tobacco. I tried it till I swallered a chaw and it made me sick. I like to died."

The girl nodded. "Ella'd be worried if she saw you now."

"Yep. Ella she done an awful lot for me." He sighed so sorrowfully that she hastily changed the subject. Tears came easy for Louie and she didn't want to have to comfort him and give him her clean handkerchief.

"What's new in town?" she asked.

"Not much. I guess you heard as the cobbler died."

"No. Poor old man. I'm sorry. I always liked him."

"I ain't sorry."

She looked at him with surprise. Louie was always so sympathetic.

He explained. "He suffered too much. Had a cancer in his stomach. A mercy he's gone."

"Oh, yes. Only I'm always sorry for anyone that has to die."

"Oh, dying's not so bad." Louie spoke authoritatively on the subject, as well he might, having buried three wives. "I mean, it ain't so bad when your time comes. It's worse looking ahead to it. Now did you ever come to think—maybe before we was born we worried because we had to be born someday, and we got born, and it wasn't so bad after all. Now we worry because we got to die, and maybe it won't be any worse than getting born. That's how I look at it."

After he was gone the girl sat thinking over his words. It was pleasant to find that poor Louie Olson believed in a fair land where unborn spirits waited to live. She wondered what other notions he might have. Next time he stopped by she planned to have a profound discussion about all manner of things.

It's as much fun to find the secret thoughts of people, she decided, as it is to try and learn the ways of wild birds and animals.

CHAPTER 4 ⟆

Joseph, the bull, was an amiable creature. He was Jersey, almost golden brown in color, with white, like milk stain, around his muzzle. His belly was light colored, the inner sides of his legs were white, so he seemed to have woolly stockings on half of every leg. Above his kind eyes were dark marks, giving him a puckish look, and he wore serious wrinkles on his brow. The girl had known him ever since he was so small that she could pick him up and carry him. That was the first week of his life. He who had been little enough to rest in her arms was now big and strong enough to kill a horse or pound a man to pulp. It amused her to look at this heavy creature and remember how weak and helpless he had been.

Though Joseph was a gentle bull, he would, as her father said, "bear watching." Of course he was different from a dairy bull that was well fed and kept in a corral. Let one of those confined animals get out and he might be mean. Joseph wasn't overfed, and he had plenty of exercise, so that helped to account for his pleasant nature.

He wasn't a noisy bull; he didn't walk along roaring and rumbling in his throat without reason as some bulls do. A neighbor had said, "That there Joseph is near as quiet as a steer."

One day Joseph started to roar until the mountain echoed his roars. A heifer in a neighbor's field was bawling for a mate. She came to the fence and for a moment it looked as if Joseph was going over the fence like an Irish hunter. The girl jumped on Pete and fought Joseph away from the fence. The heifer was scarcely a yearling; her owner wouldn't like her to be bred.

But Joseph wasn't going to settle down and graze. He muttered darkly and shook his head at Pete. The girl left it up to Pete. The old cow horse usually sensed whether an animal was bluffing or whether it meant business. Once a heifer, excited over her first calf, had used her horns on Pete and he had never forgotten. Pete was spoiled for serious work with cattle after that; he wouldn't fight to get a cow in line if he imagined the animal would charge him. It isn't often that a cow or bull will charge a horse, but once was enough for a wise pony like Pete. The old horse always considered his own safety.

Now the girl urged Pete toward the bull. If Joseph meant business, Pete would whirl out of his way. Pete had his ears flat, he stretched out his head and bit Joseph at the root of his tail. The girl could hear the sound of his teeth. Pete was calling Joseph's bluff. Either that, or Joseph was going to call Pete's bluff. Each animal was afraid of the other; the best bluffer would win the encounter. The advantage was on Pete's side, for he had started by being aggressive.

Joseph hated Pete. But that nip started him homeward to the corral where he would have to spend the rest of the day. If the bull had been kept up and well fed he would have had more vitality. He would have been with the heifer by now. As it was, he marched along the road, bellowing his dissatisfaction, shaking his head and making a few attempts to turn back. When he didn't move fast enough Pete stretched out his neck for another bite. The girl looked at the bull's shadow. It was to the side of him and a little behind, thick necked and sullen. It lagged like the spirit of Joseph.

But the next day Joseph had his triumph with a young cow whose calf was home in the barn.

A calf would be conceived by the roadside, the girl thought, and carried for nine months by its mother, until it was painfully pushed from its warm place. Then it would have to learn to stand and find nourishment. If it were a heifer it would grow to produce more of its kind. If it were a bull it would live for two months and lose its life in two minutes, and soon be eaten. All the work of a million generations so that some fat old man could say, "That was a fine roast of veal!"

Nevertheless the girl would welcome the birth of Joseph's calf. It would be August then, summer nearly gone, grass almost gray again, and the hard time coming. Calves should be born in the spring, when grass is green to make good milk. Because of a seemingly careless happening by the side of the road the girl would go out someday and find the cow in labor. Or maybe she would find the calf in the morning. Cows often had the untroublesome habit of giving birth in the night or the early morning. If the girl found the cow in labor she would watch to make sure that all was well.

Birth was a cruel thing, she thought, any way you looked at it. Being born was harder than dying, as Louie Olson had implied. But much more interesting. The girl had watched the birth of scores of calves, and hard as it was, she would rather see a calf born any day than see one killed. It was strange that birth should seem a natural process, and death so unnatural. She had often attended her cows in labor. Sometimes the poor calf would fall to the world on its head. Being limber, it seldom broke its neck, though sometimes that first meeting with the earth was a hard blow.

Then the cow, which a few minutes before had been aware of nothing in the world but pain, would turn to the calf with all love in her eyes. And what a strange rumbling moaning sound she would make, partly triumphant, partly anxious, as she watched the calf try to stand the first time.

To the girl there was more dignity in the birth of animals than of humans. Too many people existed for no other reason than the satisfaction of the flesh. The world was full of people who had accidentally been born. When you thought of it that way the cruel and foolish things they did were not so important.

At least the calves were wanted, if for no other reason than to stimulate the production of milk.

CHAPTER 5 ✒

The way one thought led to another was an odd thing. Your thoughts were connected by a chain until that chain was broken. Joseph and his mate had made her think of the many generations of bulls and cows before there could be Joseph. She had thought of the births of calves and the births of people until now she was thinking of the meeting of two people that had caused herself to be. If her father had married a different woman he would have had a child unlike herself, and where would she be? Her mother and father were unlike each other and they had produced a child that had certain characteristics of each of them, and certain feelings and ways that neither of them had. It was easy to trace the way in which she was like her mother and the way in which she was like her father. She was very glad that these two different people had united in creating her. Because of their disparities she had the ability to enjoy a variety of things.

Because an Eastern girl had visited California and fallen in love with a rancher, a child had been born who grew to enjoy what was written in books and sung in music as well as those things that were learned of earth and animals and sky.

It was really a stroke of good luck for her that these uncongenial people had happened to marry each other, though her mother's people looked on the marriage as a mistake. And for all the girl knew, there might be times when, in their secret thoughts, her mother and father thought, too, their union a mistake.

Her father would have been more successful as a rancher had he a more practical wife, one who would put up with any hardship and forego any luxury for the sake of land and cattle. In the long-ago days when it became evident that the valley would not do for cattle country because of the coming of so many small farmers, cattlemen had retreated to the high mountains. Then the girl's father had wanted to go up in the wild country, to homestead land, lease acres of range and build up a herd of good grade white-faces. The men who had gone there were wealthy now, controlling half the county's grazing. But the girl's mother had refused to leave the comfortable valley. Winters were cold in the mountains, summers were hot, falls were bitter with strong desert winds, spring came late. It might be years before she could live in a comfortable house, have a bathroom, and water running in the kitchen sink. It would be a lonely life with no near neighbors, not a store for miles, and no way to get help in a hurry should anyone fall sick.

She would have been happier if she had married a different kind of man—a teacher, perhaps, or a doctor or lawyer. A man who could give her more understanding, not one who only admired her helplessly.

She had been young when she made that Western trip and it had been romantic to marry a young rancher before her people had time to break up the affair. By the time she had been married a year she knew she had made a mistake, but no one would find it out from her. She was fond of her husband; he was gentle and kind. She knew she could have done worse, but she could have done better, too. She made a comfortable home of the old house; she was happy after the baby was born. Books and pictures and music made life a pleasant thing, and the lack of them was hard. But a living child was so much more important that those things mattered very little. Later they would achieve importance again, when she taught the child about them. When other mothers spent hoarded pennies for toys and pretty frocks, the girl's mother bought books, and when she could find a good picture that was inexpensive she bought that, too. After years of saving, a piano was brought from the city. That was a failure. The girl could not learn to play it. *Would* not, her mother said. But the child honestly tried to learn, though it was torture to practice scales when meadowlarks were whistling outside and her father was off somewhere in the fields or hills. Years later that piano was used for a down payment on a radio.

Now the girl could realize what a disappointment she must have been. Her father was proud because she was his girl, and people laughed and said, "What you really have is a son." When she was little she rode before her father in the saddle; when she grew big enough she had her own horse, Pete, who was now so old. When she wasn't riding she was following her father, her long thin legs trying to keep up with his longer ones. She even looked like her father, being lanky and gray eyed, with dark brown hair.

When she grew older her mother didn't mind telling her how disappointed she had been with her tomboy daughter. Her mother was amused at that idea now.

But for a few years it had seemed a sad and serious thing that her child was a stranger. She even went so far as to consider having more children because she so desperately wanted one who would be her very own. The fact that she even contemplated having more children showed how badly she wanted a companion, for she thought that she had nearly died when the girl was born. The old doctor had made her furious. He had said that she had had a very easy time.

Because she thought she would go insane if she had to face birth again she was careful not to have more children. But she couldn't help longing for a child with whom she could share the things she loved.

Though she lived indoors and showed little interest in the cows or horses, her experience had made her tender toward mother animals. "Poor thing," she would say of a cow heavy with calf. And a cat that was going to have kittens was brought in the house and made comfortable. When her husband laughed at her concern over brood mares and springing heifers she was cross. "What do you know about it? I'd like to see a man bear such torture!"

"Wasn't I worth it, Ma?" asked the girl, teasing her.

"Well, you are now. But for a while you weren't worth much. And I'm surprised that you've lived this long. A wonder you didn't get killed by a horse or a bull when you were little. The foolish things your father would let you do! I used to be afraid to watch you."

"Poor Ma," said the girl.

The girl could remember the day when she discovered that reading was a thing she could do for pleasure. Learning to read at school had not been fun. When she was ten years old she made one of the most important discoveries of her life.

It had been a very hot day. It was as hot as Imperial Valley, the child thought with excitement. She liked hot days. She wanted to go down to the cornfield and see the leaves all curled and droopy. Her body felt burning hot, but she liked the feeling. It was fun to walk a way in the sun and then sprawl in the shade and doze like the cows. The heat was even too much for birds and bees. There wasn't even a bumblebee humming around. The only sound was a hot weather sound, the brittle singing of cicadas hidden in the dry grass. The valley was so still, just waiting and waiting for the evening shadows. The child decided to climb trees. Leafy sycamore trees were heavenly on a day like this.

But her mother made her come into the house. "It's too hot for you to be running around. You'll have a stroke," she said.

The child was restless. On a rainy winter day it was fun to be in the house, to go from window to window and watch storms coming across the mountains. But it was hard to stay in the house when she wanted to be up among sycamore leaves.

"Settle down somewhere," her mother said. "Why don't you ever read a book?"

The child found a book that had pictures in it. The book was called *The Wind in the Willows*. Her mother had given it to her one birthday, and she had admired the pictures time and again. But reading was too slow. She looked at every picture over and over, loving them so much that she had to touch them with her fingers, tracing the outlines. After a while she knew the pictures so well she could see them with her eyes shut. These pictures were about things she knew. Little animals, and frogs in ponds. The pond pictures were lovely to look at on this hot dry day.

At last it occurred to her that maybe the printing in the book told the same sort of stories the pictures told. Slowly she began to read. She wouldn't stop reading to eat her supper. She read until her mother brought her bread and milk and made her go to bed.

She read *The Wind in the Willows* five times before her mother got her interested in another book. From that time on, whenever she wasn't riding Pete or helping her father she was somewhere reading a book.

At last she was partly her mother's child.

CHAPTER 6 ᔓ

The feeling for music had come to the girl the same way the Grace of God comes to Christians. Until then music had simply been varied sounds. All at once she had been converted to music.

It was in spring, the March of the year that she was beginning to cease being a child. It was after supper and not yet dark. She stood outside the front door, listening to the frogs piping by the river. The air was warm, smelling of mountain lilac, wild mustard and fermenting manure. She took a deep breath and thought that no earthy smell is quite as good as the smell of horse manure. The rich scrapings from the corral were spread in the flower beds and around the orange trees in the front garden. The healthy smell came through the windows, you breathed it when you went to sleep and when you woke up in the morning, and it spoke of the fecundity of damp earth in the spring.

A mockingbird started to sing with all its might, and she listened to it until the frog singing was only a quivering background for the bird's song. Quite near she heard the soft excited squeak of a bat. Like a flash she saw the arched wings in the dim air. It darted soundlessly and vanished.

She heard her mother moving around in the living room, and then her mother began to play the piano there in the darkness. The girl wasn't consciously listening to the piano. She stood looking at the first star and not thinking of anything in particular.

She became aware that she was tense, listening, half holding her breath. Her ears caught sounds automatically, but it was with her mind that she was listening. She had no idea what it was her mother was playing, she had never heard it before. It might be that her mother was making it up as she went along. It didn't matter.

The girl hadn't the slightest idea what the music was trying to say. It made her vaguely sorrowful and vaguely happy. It made her think of the earth's bright past, of old pictures and young men. She longed for something without knowing what she longed for. She grieved for the dead, she sorrowed for the living. For once she felt an all-embracing tenderness for the world and everything in it. For bewildered people with all their cruelties and lusts. For animals and trees, mountains and deserts. For the land she knew and the cities she might never know. For oceans and rivers, for skies and stars. She spread out her arms. The first star became fragments before her tears. It split into a million drops of light. The music was unmerciful.

Then it stopped, but still she heard it. In a minute her mother would speak to her, and she couldn't bear it. She ran down the garden path. In the barn the first spring calf was with its mother. In there it was dark, and the bodies of the cow and calf were heavy with warmth. She spoke so she wouldn't startle the cow. She crept on her knees and found the soft calf. She held its sleepy head in her arms.

Underneath it the straw was damp and warm. The wet straw smelled good; it held the smell of a young body. She felt the calf's heart beat; she breathed breath for breath as it did. She heard the cow chewing her cud, heard her swallowing moistly, heard her gulp up a fresh cud, sigh gustily with sleepiness.

The girl felt her body relax like the animals'. The remembered tones of music grew dimmer.

She went to sleep and woke up hearing her name called. Her mother and father were cross because she had disappeared and had frightened them. It was very late. How silly for a great girl to go off to sleep with a calf, they said.

She didn't answer them. There was no explanation they could understand. She walked to the house with dignity, undressed and went to bed. But forever afterward she felt the need of music. She loved it, but it tormented her. Music spoke of too many things. It was disturbing and confusing. There were times when she had to hear it, when she longed for the colored sounds of operas and symphonies. But music wasn't for every day. It was meant to be taken as some people take religion.

There were enough other things for every day.

The sound of music and the words in books were good things to have, and cattle and horses and fields were part of living.

CHAPTER 7 ✎

She could remember how the conviction came to her that of all animals on earth, the human animal is the least beautiful.

Some years ago, on a November day, her father said that one thing he wasn't going to miss this time was the yearling trials of thoroughbred horses. The races took place on a big ranch, half a day's journey away.

The girl remembered every bit of that day. They all hurried in the morning to get an early start, and as they traveled her father explained about the custom of throwing the ranch gates open to the public one day in the year. It was a custom brought down from the old Spanish times in California when the ranch owners invited the whole countryside to come and feast, and admire fine cattle and horses. It was a great and wonderful thing, her father said, that this fine old tradition still existed. You won't find anything like it in the world, except here in California.

November Grass

They drove through yellow valleys and over sun-browned hills, and by noon they reached the whitewashed fences of the horse ranch. It was in a small valley, hill enfolded. In rolling pastures mares and big colts rested under live oaks.

They drove right up to the ranch house as if they owned it, which indeed, everyone did that day. A tall man smiled and welcomed them, and said that the barbecued beef and Mexican beans were ready, to go where tables were under the trees, and to help themselves.

When the girl was served with a plate of food, she couldn't eat. For in a small ring young horses were being led around in preparation for the first run of the afternoon. One burning sorrel would dance three steps and then lash out with his hind feet. He simply couldn't wait for the race to begin. There were four horses in the ring, and all of them minced and tossed their high heads, and the sunshine was fiery on their coats. But the girl took the sorrel to her heart. She felt she couldn't bear it if he were not the swiftest.

After everyone was through eating a bell rang, and the people sat on the ground where they could get a good view of the track. The excited colts, ridden by boys, were coaxed into the starting gate. A bell rang again, the riders shouted, the colts stretched out and ran.

It was such a bright and beautiful thing to see that she felt tears in her eyes. And she shouted with all her heart when the sorrel sprinted ahead of them all.

That was only the beginning. She saw so much loveliness that afternoon that her heart began to beat as fast as the hearts of the racing colts. She wandered through the big barns and cupped the noses of thoroughbreds in her hands, stroked curved necks, looked deep into deep eyes.

For a long while she didn't notice the people who crowded the barns and stretched out hands to the friendly horses.

After each run the colts were led into a barn where there was space for them to be walked and cooled. People sat on bales of hay and leaned against the sides of stalls and looked at the horses with great seriousness. The girl realized that she had never seen such a well-behaved crowd. No one spoke too loudly or moved suddenly; it was as though they understood that they were in the presence of something like royalty.

But for all their good manners the people were looking at the animals critically. A fat man pointed almost triumphantly to a splint on the leg of a tall rangy bay. It was so small a blemish that it was hardly noticeable. Anyway, the young horse would probably outgrow it.

The girl stared coldly at the big man. It wasn't right that anyone with so imperfect a body as his should feel superior about a slight defect in a gorgeously built animal.

She looked at the horses and looked at the people. How ugly they would look without their clothes. Skins the color of white grubs in the earth. Paunchy fronts and fat rears. Or else scrawny bodies—like her own—showing too much bony structure. Even the best built of the humans could not compare with the animals.

She decided the trouble was that the humans had too many small protruding parts. The insects that people consider the most repulsive have many small parts. Humans have the same fault. Arms that move around every way, flexible hands, little jointed fingers. Faces broken by small features, too many visible parts to the ear. Heads abruptly joined to necks, necks to chests.

The beasts were compact, one part moulding beautifully into another. No noses sticking out from the face. Plainly made ears that were able to catch sound better than human ears. Beautifully spaced eyes and noble brow. No abrupt joining of head and neck, neck and chest. A horse, even the least beautiful, was a series of curved lines. And humans were either angular, or bulging with misplaced fat.

She felt ashamed. She thought of other animals. Yes, man was better looking than a hippopotamus, or a pig. But a newborn pig was handsomer and smarter than a newborn human. Still, compared with horses and cattle, deer and coyotes, lions and tigers and certain birds, man didn't look like much at all.

It had certainly been clever of him to overcome his physical handicaps and rule the world the way he did.

CHAPTER 8 ⌢

The road where the girl herded her cows was about twelve miles long. Westward it went to the main highway, eastward it went to mountain country. There it branched, one branch going to the Indian reservation, one branch climbing to Ricardo's Ranch halfway up a mountain. The road going to the reservation connected with a wider better road on the other side of the valley. The Indians who drove cars, and they were many, used the better road. The ones who rode or drove their ponies used the quieter road. It was a beautiful road because, so far, the county had not tried to improve it. It followed the way of the river and the way of the hill, so it was obliged to bend this way and that and dodge trees and boulders.

Where canyons opened toward the river and creeks flowed in winter there were wooden bridges with white rails. The dry summers made the bridges rattle when cars or horses crossed them. There were four little bridges, one for Lost Horse Canyon, one for Coyote Canyon, one for Fernstone Canyon and one for Chicken Hawk Canyon. The canyons were rough draws parting the hills, used for pastures. They hardly called for names, but the girl was glad they had names, for she liked the sound of them. In a few weeks the cattle would have grazed their way down the road as far as Lost Horse Canyon. There she could sit on the white rail of the bridge and watch them. The road was fenced on both sides down there, so the cows would have only narrow strips for grazing.

Seven families lived along the road. The girl's father could remember when the road served only his own ranch, when he had most of the valley and hills for his cattle. He said California was a good land before too many people came. Now there were fences and gardens and chicken farms where there had been open range. Instead of a big herd of beef cattle he had these few old cows, and heifers he raised to sell as milk cows. He had hogs and chickens and turkeys and the big field and the little field, for corn and oats. Six hundred and forty acres he had left out of all the hills and valley, and not many of those acres were fit for cultivation. Most of the land was hill pasture, now inhabited by an old stallion and four mares. They were lean because they had to travel so far from water to grass. But they would make out all right. They weren't like cows—the cows wouldn't climb hills and hunt for grass when it was sparse in the fall.

The neighbors were not even so well off as her father. A few cows, a work team, chickens, turkeys and pigs. Some of the men hired out to plow and do odd jobs, a few worked as milkers on dairies. Their children were clean and had enough to eat. They went to school in a yellow bus along with the Indian children.

Sometimes it seemed long ago since the girl had ridden in that yellow bus. Sometimes it seemed only a month or two ago. From September until June, five days a week, for twelve years she had been a passenger. Toward the last the bus had seemed like a monster that gobbled up children along the way and spewed them out in the school yard. Happy children and sad children, quarreling children and friendly children. Sometimes the children screamed and laughed all the way; sometimes they united in teasing some unfavored companion; sometimes two boys would quarrel so violently they came to blows. Then the driver would stop and make the fighting ones get out and walk.

Through rain and sun, heat and cold that bus trundled back and forth, its belly full of weeping, laughing, helpless children. In September the six-year-olds boarded it for the first time. Their mothers would come to the bus stop with them, hand them their new lunch boxes, and start them on their first journey to school. The little ones would ride, quiet and solemn eyed, clutching the shining lunch boxes, awed at the older ones who had made this trip so often. Some of them cried. But after a while the newness wore off, they bickered among themselves, they traded pencils and erasers.

The girl could remember those rides in the bus more vividly than she could remember the days in the classroom. Now she was glad all that was over for her. Let people talk of carefree happy childhood. Their memories must be short. A child can be intensely happy, but adults never feel the depths of despair and misery a troubled child can know. A child can be worried and humiliated out of all proportion to the cause of its discomfort. A child can know terror vivid enough to drive an older person half insane.

What thinking woman could sigh wistfully and wish to be sixteen again? The girl could laugh at that tremulous uncertain time, but still she could remember the perplexi ties and fears. Being a tall brown girl she had wished to be small and golden and white. Before a school dance her dress had been lovely as a willow tree, but once she arrived and compared it with the others it ceased to look right. What if no one asked her to dance? What if she had to sit by the teacher who chaperoned, staring brightly at the happy girls who had partners? The agony was so intense that it hurt to her bones. Every detail of living was too important in those days. She would never wish to be sixteen again.

The things she had learned in classes faded from her mind like old dreams. The history dates she had had to stay after class and memorize—not one did she know now. Algebra and Latin, how she had struggled to learn what she had so completely forgotten! But she still remembered the face of her first beau, and her agony of jealousy when he grew to like another girl better. Now she could laugh at what had been tragedy. Remembering, she stretched luxuriantly in the grass and looked with pleased eyes at the world. It was good to be a grown woman, twenty-three years old.

But the things she had learned from earth and animals would always be part of her life. Those things hadn't been learned like lessons, they had been absorbed. She knew the mountain by heart so she could walk on it at night. She knew where there were mortar holes in the stones where Indians had pounded acorns into meal. She knew every hidden spring, every box canyon, the remote spots where chocolate bells grew in the spring. She knew the particular scent and look of everything that grew on the brushy mountain. She knew the geography of hill country, where likely there would be ridges, draws or hogbacks, so if she rode in unfamiliar places she could tell where there might be a trail, or a fairly easy way to get down to a valley. From a high place she could look into a canyon, read the signs from vegetation, trails or the color of the earth, and say for sure whether or not there would be water there.

She knew how the south wind would bring rain, and how the earth would take it, smoothly in some places, in others holding it under the surface in hidden reservoirs, so her horse would flounder in a bog before she knew it. She knew how the grass would start to dry in May, holding a rich golden color half the summer, then fading to gray as the sun scorched the strength from it—until by fall there was little nourishment in it, and cattle and horses had to eat three times as much as they did in early summer, so that they grew potbellied from too much roughage.

She knew the timid way of a colt when it is afraid of people, but still, in spite of itself, interested in the process of being gentled. She remembered how a colt put out its trembling nose, daring to touch her, but afraid to let her hand touch its face. How, if a stranger came near, it crowded close to her, afraid of being touched, but more afraid of the unknown. And how at last she knew she had its confidence when she could rub the folded nostrils that still quivered under her fingers. The girl could feel her way with the colt's shy mind until she worked with the colt subjectively instead of objectively. Then she owned the colt completely, as completely as she owned the filly that grazed beside old Pete.

She could shut her eyes and see nearly every calf that had been born on the place as long as she was old enough to remember. Her hands knew the feel of their wet newborn bodies; her arms and back knew the soft weight of them when she carried them to the barn. She could feel the calf's struggle as it stood up that first time. She knew the confiding look of young eyes; calves had a false sense of security, a feeling that their mothers could protect them always. It was a pitiful thing when you knew that their big deep-bellied mothers were as helpless as the newborn before the decisions of their masters. Before a calf was dry a cattle buyer might load it in his truck and take it off to be fattened for veal.

Man was the enemy of all creatures: his domestic beasts he tended for his own profit, the wild ones he destroyed for his pleasure. The girl, who had no wish to kill, could track a deer or find a coyote as well as any hunter. She knew where the deer came to drink, she could tell where one had bedded down at night. In the spring she hunted fawns for the pleasure of seeing them. Hunting for hidden calves had taught her how to find fawns. Where she might least expect to see one, there it would be, in a brushy place where shadows and sun matched the markings of its coat. If it wasn't startled it would lie and look at her out of big accepting eyes. It accepted the sight of a quiet human as it accepted the sight of rocks and brush. She never touched one, never defiled it with human scent.

If she looked at its beauty until she remembered it always, then she had it to keep. It was hers as it wouldn't be if she stole it from its hiding place and took it home to raise. It would not be her fawn then; it would grow to be a buck or a doe, be restless for the hills and wander away, maybe to be killed by a hunter. She felt she owned it if she saw it completely as the little fawn, always the young fawn waiting for its mother. The doe would be back to care for it. A person who did not know the habit of a doe might think the fawn deserted, but the mother was grazing somewhere, not once forgetting where her fawn rested.

Coyote pups were charming, too. The girl had hidden where the wind blew toward her and watched five puppies playing in the sun. The mother had scratched out a shallow burrow in the hillside. She lay by her low doorway and the children crawled over her, bit at each other, and sucked at her dark nipples. When they grew a little stronger she would take them hunting. Then she would need to be more alert than ever with the five of them to be watched every minute.

At night the girl liked to listen to coyotes. Sometimes they barked with questioning voices, sometimes they wailed, sometimes she knew they were hunting and the trail was hot.

About earth and animals she felt she knew a great deal. About her own kind she knew little. But sometimes she liked to think about her neighbors, and speculate about the way they must feel. She didn't know many people, just the sort who lived hereabouts. From books she knew of an entirely different type of human being. She wondered if she would ever leave this place and see other things. Sometimes she thought she wanted to, again she shrank from the idea of the unfamiliar. For a long time she had identified herself with the things she knew; she was not sure what she would be if she ever went to a new place.

CHAPTER 9 ⇜

When the girl went to the city she liked to go to the depot and see the trains pull out and watch the people. Someday she was going to see the new streamliner that went north. But from what they said about it she thought she wouldn't like it. It didn't snort out smoke and start off with an effort that made its going seem important, as the old trains did. They said it pulled out so smoothly there was scarcely a sound. Riding on it wouldn't seem like riding on a train at all.

But whether the train was new fashioned or old, the travelers would act the same. The girl liked watching people embrace the home-coming and bid good-bye to those about to leave. She always wondered about the people she saw there, where they were going and why.

It would be pretty bad to travel if it grieved you to part with people. It would be a sorrowful thing to be going away from everything you loved.

November Grass

The girl thought that she wouldn't want to be away for long, but just once she would like to go away on a train and see how it would feel.

Yet while other people were going and coming, somehow seeming to evade time, the girl had traveled in a small world, starting out each day, returning to the same berth each night. It was as if she had been journeying through the seasons, and fall was the stopping place each year. Now she was waiting for rains to start the season moving.

She liked the idea of staying a lifetime in one place. It was more satisfying to know well one small part of the earth than to have sketchy knowledge of a hundred places. People who moved about a great deal must find their lives marked sharply into separate periods of time and place. Boyhood must seem far away to a man who has lived in many different houses. He must feel sadness and a sense of loss when he visited scenes where he used to play.

Life, she felt, is like a long unbroken line when one dies in the same place in which he was born. Childhood doesn't seem long ago when every day a man sees the same things he saw the first time he began to look around. Then there can't seem such a sharp division between youth and age. A person would grow into his years like a tree.

If the girl lived here to become an old woman everything she saw would have a meaning. About each stone and tree she might remember something she had thought or done. The days when she had been little would not seem sorrowfully distant. All her life would be wrapped around her; she would feel safe and warm. All her days added together would seem many, yet no part of them would be lost in time and far-away places.

In her narrow traveling she had become well acquainted with hills and fields, winding roads, country people, animals and the changing scene of weather. When spring came this road would be as different as if it were in another land; as if, when you followed it, it took you to some altogether new place. Leaves wore a young color. In place of dusty golden-rod there would be yellow wild mustard, very sweet smelling, and wild pink roses would start to bloom.

Grain fields would be so shining green that when you went through them and the sun was low you would see a halo shining around the shadow of your head.

And all along the ways of country roads there would be new sights in the pastures. Colts, and so many calves that invariably the price of veal went down in the spring. Spring looked so gay and happy that the girl forgot what a sorrowful time it was. It was a hard thing to think of calves in terms of veal and the happy lambs as ultimate roast meat. With all the earth so tender why did mankind show so lit-tle compassion for mother animals and their young?

Long before she saw enough of mountain lilacs and running streams and ferny hollows in the hills the road traveled into summer.

But that was a good time, too. A time of beautiful browns on the hills and pockets of green in the valleys. Long hot days shaded into nights soft with the cry of poor-wills and killdeer and owls. During summer days birds were quieter than in spring, but when canyons cooled with shadow the wrens sang, and they started up the others.

November Grass

There was so much of summer which the girl forgot when she was in winter, and so much of winter which she forgot when she was in summer, that each time she went through a season it held new pleasures for her. The girl enjoyed every spring as much as if it were the first spring come to earth. The smell of cut hay was always sweeter than she remembered. The air of early summer brought a smell of drying flowers, and as evening came the damp places by the river had a lush fragrance unlike any other. Then every fall came the rain after over half a year of drought, and the sound of rain, and the smell of wet dust brought such intense delight that the long drought was worth having if for no other reason than the joy of its ending.

Traveling with her, and feeling each season as intensely as she felt it, were the animals. From Pete to Flaxie, from old Whitey cow to the youngest calf, the animals were aware of changes in earth and sky. Bad weather they endured with rumps to storms; cold clear nights made them love the morning sun. They sensed the coming of rain so strongly that even the heaviest cows would gallop and kick up their heels when dampness freshened the air. Like the girl they felt better in spring and early summer. Of course there was an obvious reason for their pleasure; grass was so plentiful that the sorriest animal couldn't help sprucing up. But there was something else. Sometimes the girl thought that animals, especially lambs and kids, calves and colts, got vibrations of unheard music from the earth itself—for often, their caperings were in rhythm as perfect as dance patterns. They might be keeping time to melodies that grass roots knew. The mother animals, too, felt it at certain times; they cavorted when they remembered the fun of being young.

The girl felt sure that she would never grow too old and weary to feel glad at each turning of the season. She would have an eternal interest in earth and sky, though each spring and summer, fall and winter was bringing her nearer to the time when time must end for her. It is said that we live in the midst of death, and the girl thought she was happy in the midst of sorrow. To a certain extent the future can be read. The girl knew for sure that times would come when she would be darkly troubled. That is the odd thing about living, she thought. You can be happy one day though you know that on another you will feel as if you cannot bear to live.

CHAPTER 10 ✐

At night, too, the road was different, leading to a different land. It was in summer that the girl knew the night road best.

After long hot days it was better to ride in the night than sleep. Late in the afternoon mountain shadows cooled the road, and between sunset and darkness was the time to start out. Then faint apricot color was in the sky toward the west, and the poor-will birds cried compassionately and nestled in the road ahead, and flew up before the horse to drop down a few feet further on. Their wings made not the slightest sound at all; the birds moved with such a softness that not even shadows could be quieter.

Bats allowed themselves to be outlined on the sky for only brief glimpses, and they were soundless, too. Voices of owls were muted; the only sharp-crying birds were killdeer.

After the sky looked quite dark everywhere else there was still a light mark outlining the crests of hills, as if the half-light loved hills even more than the stars did.

The coming of a summer night is so tender that the girl felt then that she could not bear summer to end. It was as though she had an appointment with a lover at a certain hour each evening. It was an hour to which she looked forward all through the day.

She could never decide which nights she liked better—the gray nights of starlight, or the amber nights of moonlight. She could see very well in starlight after she had been out in it a while. Of all growing things the wild-tobacco bushes looked most beautiful in starlight. Each leaf and blossom and twig was clean against the sky. There wasn't an ungraceful line. Oak trees were thick dark blurs, and sycamores were little better. Cottonwoods had to have moonlight to be at their best. Willows made a good pattern any time. But to see a dead tree groping toward the moon was the most beautiful thing of all.

Cattle and horses were enchanted creatures on a moonlight night. A plow horse resting in pasture looked like a noble charger fit to carry a prince. Cows became sacred beasts, walking in beauty.

One night the girl made a chain of garden flowers and decorated Joseph, the bull, like a sacrificial ox. He was very patient and kind while she entwined his horns with leaves and blossoms. When she was done he walked slowly and proudly as if he didn't want to shake off a petal. He was dignified and beautiful in the moonlight. When morning came he still wore some of his finery. Then he looked ridiculous.

Sometimes on a warm night the wind would come like a wanderer and set everything in motion, and the smell of the wind was like the desert—sharp and sweet, and there was a sadness about it.

At night little houses against the hills looked pitiful. When you thought about people, you thought of them as lost among the stars. Then the road was a small pathway leading to nowhere.

CHAPTER 11 ⬎

One summer night she followed the road to the Indian reservation. It was August, the month of the corn moon, and the Indians were having a fiesta.

The reservation was a small one, and it was said that the Indians were all sick. Some of the older ones could no longer see. The younger ones thought of nothing but owning automobiles and drinking whisky. But every year when August came they remembered that it was time for harvest ceremonies. So then they invited Indians from other reservations to join them, and they invited white people to come watch them celebrate.

They had electric lights and they had a dance platform and they had a jazz orchestra. They had booths where people spun wheels for Kewpie dolls and colored balloons. They had booths where hot dogs and soda pop and ice-cream cones were sold. Little Indian girls in gingham dresses and little Indian boys in overalls darted through the crowds and thought that everything was beautiful and exciting. The very old Indians simply sat staring at whatever they chanced to see. The young people couldn't relax for a minute, they were busy acting like ordinary American young people. They danced to the jazz music and drank red soda pop and spoke nothing but American slang. The Indian girls had permanent waves, their cheeks and lips were bright with rouge. They wore thin dresses and high-heeled slippers. The old Indians and the young Indians seemed like separate races.

After a while half a dozen old men moved apart and built a little fire on the ground. Then some of the women came and put down a few ears of corn, a watermelon and some sacks of Bull Durham tobacco.

While their sons and daughters danced to orchestra music, three old men began to chant. Without seeming to open their mouths at all some old women took up the chant. One old woman stood leaning on a cane. She had a fine thin face. Her bones looked aristocratic. Some of the women had coarse features, but this old woman was beautiful. She stood away from the others, and shadows from the fire crossed her face.

The old men began to dance, and hardly anyone noticed them. They stamped around the fire, looking shabby in their overalls. Because they didn't wear tribal costumes or feathers the girl was impressed by their sincerity. This was no exhibition of ceremonial dances. This was a religious rite performed in sadness because it was soon to be forgotten. The orchestra drowned out the rhythm of the chanting. The old men must have had to concentrate fiercely in order to dance at all.

A few people finally gathered around to watch them. The young Indians looked as amused as the white people. It was very funny to see those old men going around the fire. The orchestra continued playing jazz.

The girl looked at the beautiful old Indian woman. She had turned her face toward the stars. Her eyes were shut. She swayed a little and there was rapture on her face. She did not hear the jazz. She heard only the chanting of her own voice. She had better listen while she could. The time was fast coming when the sound of Indian chanting would never rise toward the stars.

After a while the men stopped chanting and looked sheepish. The jazz notes filled the air; the orchestra had won. It was then that the girl felt one of those sad little winds rustle the air, and it was like the ghosts of gods departing.

CHAPTER 12 ꙮ

Some of the people the girl liked best were Mexicans.
Mexicans fitted as well as Indians into this semidesert
country. They had an unhurried way of living that was like
the slow way of summer turning toward autumn. They had
a gaiety that was like April. They liked to sleep and they
liked to sing and they didn't like to worry. Even the poor-
est were gracious, and their hospitality was genuine.

Mamá and Papá Gonzalez were special friends of the
girl's. She never rode by their little house without stopping
to talk awhile, and Mamá Gonzalez was never too busy to
talk. Mamá Gonzalez was never too busy to do what she
wanted. She would stop in the middle of hanging a wash
on the line if she felt like writing a poem.

The girl wished she could read Spanish so she could
understand Mamá's poems. They sounded lovely when
Mamá read them to her. The rhythm of the Spanish was
like flowing water.

The girl would ask Mamá to translate. "It does not sound so good in English," Mamá would say apologetically. She would frown as she studied over a verse, trying to think it into English. "It is about this girl and she loves greatly a man. He is a bullfighter and he is killed and the girl cries out how though her lover is dead her love will live forever. You understand? Though the people who love die, love itself does not die. So this girl, she thinks of that."

"It is very beautiful," the girl said.

Mamá Gonzalez nodded. "Yes, and true. I know."

The girl looked a little wonderingly at Mamá Gonzalez, who was an old woman. She had had nine children and they all had families of their own now, except the most beautiful, a girl who had died. Mamá often spoke of her. Her name was Margarita. Margarita had been too good and beautiful to last.

But though all their children had gone away, the Gonzalezes were not lonely. They had many good friends and they had a large family of animals. The animals liked to gather around the house, and when Mamá and Papá Gonzalez sat outdoors on Sunday afternoons there were the gentle cows and heifers standing about; Carlos the red bull; the old plow horse, Pancho; the chickens and turkeys; Rosita the white goat; and the dogs and cats. Sometimes their friends came calling on those afternoons and the yard was full of laughing people and sleepy animals.

One day Mamá Gonzalez called the girl to come see what Rosita had done. Rosita had had four white kids.

"So many," said Mamá proudly. "Three she might have had, but four, is it not a miracle?"

November Grass

The girl agreed that it was a miracle. The day-old kids were strong and lively. Already they were playing. "They bounded around like grasshoppers," Mamá said admiringly. They wanted to climb on everything, as if they knew that goats love high mountain ledges. Little goats, from the minute they are born, know exactly how to be goats.

Rosita, acting delightfully astonished, kept bleating to them, and they answered in quavering trebles. Like her, they were all white.

"Three Nannies and the one Beelly," said Mamá Gonzalez. "He is Jesus, and this is Anita. Lily, we call this, and the small one is Dolores. Look at that Rosita. So much milk."

But though Rosita gave quantities of milk, four growing kids drank more than one goat could make. To help her out, Mamá fed the kids cow's milk from a bottle. In a day or two the kids accepted the fact that they had two mothers, and they trooped after Mamá Gonzalez as eagerly as they followed Rosita.

When Mamá stepped out the kitchen door the four little goats gathered around to nibble her fingers and pull at her apron strings. They followed her to the outhouse, and stood peeking through the cracks and crying imploringly.

Mamá was very proud of them.

One Sunday afternoon the girl stopped by to talk awhile.

Mamá and Papá, dressed in Sunday clothes, had their chairs under a tree, and as usual the animals were gathered around. One of the little goats was asleep in Mamá's lap, two more rested by her chair.

Papá Gonzalez stood up to give the girl his chair.

"A beautiful day," the girl said, and Mamá and Papá agreed. The girl looked around. "Why, where's the little Billy goat?"

Mamá sighed, and touched her eyes with a white handkerchief. "We feel bad, almost as if we had lost a *niño.*"

"Mamá, you will write a little poem about him someday," said Papá Gonzalez consolingly.

To the girl he explained. "We ate the little Beelly Jesus for our dinner."

CHAPTER 13 ⌒

She was half asleep by the road while her cows were grazing, when a car came slowly by and stopped. In it were two girls she had known at school.

"Guess what," said the taller one, "Molly is going to be married!"

Molly held her left hand so that the sun sparkled on a diamond.

"Well!" The girl hardly knew what to say. "That's fine, Molly. Who is he?"

He was a boy Molly had known all her days. The girl wondered how Molly could be so excited.

"It's a funny thing," Molly declared. "I'd known him so long and never thought much about him. He took me to a movie and we went to some dances. I don't know how it happened. All of a suddenlike, we fell in love. And we think we can have our wedding on Christmas."

The girls sat down in the shade.

"Time you married and settled down," said Molly to the girl.

"I'm already settled down. You don't have to get married to do that."

The girls looked interested. "Who are you going with?"

"No one. Who would there be to go with here? I mean I'm settled down, contented, happy."

"Oh, the right one will come along someday," said Molly.

"Let him come," said the girl, "I don't care one way or the other. Marriage is all right, but I can be happy anyway."

The tall girl said, "Every normal woman wants a home of her own. Aren't you normal?"

The girl laughed. "I guess every woman thinks she wants babies, too. I don't."

Molly was horrified.

"All right, Molly. But you haven't seen as many cows have calves as I have."

Molly shuddered. "But that's different."

"No, it isn't. It's the same whether it's a cow or a bitch or a mare or a sow or a woman."

The tall girl explained. "But bearing a child is only a small part of it. Look at the pleasure you'd get out of your babies."

"Yes, and look at the worry. I don't think mothers are so happy. Lots of children are disappointing. And when you are old and need them they're busy with families of their own."

"That's life," said Molly. "And I should think you'd feel as though you were missing something, the way you live. I think it's awful lonesome in this valley."

Am I missing something? thought the girl. But she didn't say anything. Certainly she wasn't lonely. Once in a great while she grew restless, especially when she thought of last summer. But then she had felt that way before, in the spring. She remembered how certain music heard over the radio had made her feel as though she were homesick for a place she had never seen. A mare had galloped across the pasture and had stopped to look far off and whinny. The girl had laughed. "I'm just like the rest of nature," she had said to herself. Then, having recognized the cause of her discontent, she had grown tranquil again.

"Molly," she said, "you're like a young heifer."

But Molly didn't understand.

"Look," pointed the girl, and laughed aloud.

A heifer stood staring at them. The heifer was fat and blonde like Molly, and had Molly's same wondering expression.

Molly glanced at the heifer but she did not look amused.

CHAPTER 14 ❧

It had been fun to amaze Molly by speaking disparagingly of marriage. But it was only a brief time ago that the girl herself had wanted to be married. It was a queer thing to think about now that she followed such a strict routine every day. It seemed as if her life had never been different, as if it never would change. She didn't want it to change, she thought, really, but there were certain things about last summer that were hurtful to remember. Sweetly hurtful, not sharply so. Just a short time ago it had seemed a sharp thing, but sometimes now it seemed only a half-remembered dream. Yet it could become vivid and painful again.

Right now, if Dirk should come walking up the road, the girl would be helpless. The sun shining on his red head would make her want to stretch out her hands as toward a fire. The sight of his clumsy gangling figure would make her feel tender as a mother. She could admit that now very calmly. It was simply a fact. It was all something that happened and had become part of her life, and she knew it was something that couldn't be helped. She had fought against it for a while, then come to accept it as you accept the knowledge of anything that is true. You grow used to everything. The girl could think without excitement, "I wanted Dirk, but apparently he didn't want me."

The girl knew that in most cases people fall in love and marry because of circumstance. Young people affianced are likely to think that marriage is something like destiny. Yet most young people fall in love with the most convenient person who happens to be around.

But she always thought that in her case it was different. None of the men she happened to know would suit her at all. She wanted someone whose thoughts were like her own. She was sure that there were few men in all the world, perhaps only one, that would be suitable for her. She could not be content if her mind was filled with domestic affairs only. She wanted to think of something besides clothes and babies and cooking.

Dirk came from a little town in Kansas. He came to look at the strangeness of mountain and desert and sea. And in everything he saw there was music. Now to many people there is music in the sea and the wind in the branches and the sound of bird wings. But Dirk felt symphonies in mountain ranges. The desert was metallic music and soft little valleys were love songs. Dirk had a lot in common with the ancient who wrote of the morning stars singing together.

Dirk stayed across the valley with his aunt and uncle. He was not like them at all. He was not like anyone else the girl had ever known.

It so happened that when the young people gathered for dances or beach parties or picnics or hayrides the girl and Dirk were paired off together. It seemed to happen naturally. Dirk said most of the girls were discords. They didn't belong in this valley at all; they would be in tune only in the city. But the girl belonged here. Her presence seemed to satisfy him.

The more they talked the more they found to talk about. The girl had never spoken so fully to anyone as she had to Dirk. They could be silent together, too.

Except for his eyes and hands Dirk was not a good-looking man. With his red hair and fair skin you would expect Dirk to have blue eyes, or green. Instead his eyes were brown. They were never dull. When the girl talked she felt as if Dirk was listening with his eyes as well as his ears. His eyes said words, too. They seemed to be eager approving words.

His hands were large. But not like the broad hands of the boys who milked cows. They were strong long-fingered hands; you would expect a sculptor to have them. When she was not with him the girl thought about his hands even more than she did his eyes. She wanted to hold them in her own calloused unbeautiful hands.

It came to her slowly that she loved him. It did not disturb her. She had been waiting, and now the thing she had waited for had come. She was glad. But she didn't go about daydreaming and sighing, nor did she notice that her heartbeats quickened. She didn't know how things would work out, but she didn't worry. Dirk had one more year of studying, then he would have to find a job teaching music in some high school. That job would make his life secure financially so that he could write music. The girl knew that he would be a very great composer.

CHAPTER 15 ☙

One day Dirk went alone on a pilgrimage. He went off by himself to look at the ocean. The girl had never realized what a great thing the ocean is in the imaginations of people who have never seen it. People live and die without seeing it, but always hoping someday to make a journey to the shore. Dirk taught her something new about the ocean.

She had never especially loved the sea because it had been associated in her mind with the beach. The beach, with its few beautiful brown people and its scores of repulsive pink people, its noise and its smell and its glare—the girl felt only disgust when she was there.

Dirk saw nothing but the clean water rising to the clean sky. He heard nothing but the rhythm of waves. He studied the waves and saw how one side of them was like the underside of water, how one side was like surface water, and how the crests were yet a different thing.

He said, "All that water, and nothing can ever happen to it. The ocean is one thing people can't harm. They can

cross it in ships, or fly over it, but they can't leave any last-
ing impression on it. They plow up land and the wind
blows it away, they chop down forests and mountainsides
erode, but they can't do anything to the ocean. A big
storm comes along, and after it's over the water is the same
again. It is the one savage and primitive thing left in nature.
That's why I like it."

Then the girl loved the water. After Dirk had made
that first pilgrimage alone he took the girl and walked
along the shore until there was no more smooth sand, and
no sound of shouting people. They climbed cliffs and saw
dark cormorants and white seagulls and gray pelicans. They
listened to the surge of water and the calling of birds.

Somehow it pleased the girl because Dirk became
unaware of her. Compared to waves and cliffs and birds and
clouds she was of no interest whatever. He forgot to turn
and help her over steep places. She followed him, feeling as
humble as a little sister tagging after a tall brother.

Then on a clear hot day they took a trail over the
hills. She had to show him the sea as she loved it best. He
rode an enormous work mare, the girl rode old Pete, and
because of the weather they stopped often to rest their
mounts. Being from the Middle West he was used to summer heat, and the girl liked the warmest days. The sun
sharpened the smell of sagebrush and buckwheat and the
sweat of horses. The hill country looked arid, and Dirk,
used to flat rich fields, found it powerfully beautiful.

It was past noon before they reached the grassy mesa
the girl had in mind. So the sun was very bright, and at the

right angle to make a shining field of the water many miles away. At first Dirk said it was a fog bank, for it looked vertical. The girl pointed out that a fog bank would not have so even an edge. "Anyway," she said, "ships don't ride on fog banks." She had to show him the ship. Between two hills, it was a dark blur on the water field. But the longer they looked, the more perfectly it became a ship. And far out was the corpselike shape of an island.

To look between mountains at the ocean is to see it the best way, and Dirk admitted it, and was pleased with her for showing it to him. So the girl felt pleased with herself, as though she had done a great and wonderful thing; she felt deserving of award.

They ate sandwiches and stretched out in the shade of a boulder and talked while the horses grazed on the dry bunchgrass. They talked of all things, of death and war and birth and trees and animals and themselves. Dirk said there would be war. And, in the brightness of that high place, it did not seem true. "That ship," said Dirk, "isn't it likely to be a warship?" And the girl looked at what had been a dark blur, and the outlines became clear, and it was wrong that there should be such a warlike thing in the midst of peace.

"But you wouldn't go to war," she told him.

He said he would. "I wouldn't be brave enough to refuse. I'd hate it, but I'd have to go."

The girl didn't dare look at him then. He mustn't see how the thought was almost more than she could stand, how war had suddenly become a terrible and personal thing to her.

"You don't want to die," she told him.

"I don't want to. But it doesn't fill me with any great horror. No one has any choice in the matter; it is part of living, in a way. I'm not afraid of it, though I don't like it."

The girl said how she hated and feared death above all things. "You haven't seen as much of it as I have. Things have died while I loved them, while I've tried to hold them back with my arms around them tight. It is horrible." She spoke of the bloated bodies of dead horses, and how, when you roll a calf over into a grave, gurgling sounds will be in its throat, after it has been dead for hours.

"But that isn't death. That's just what is left over from living. When you are dead you won't even know that you are dead. Like sleeping without dreaming. Or being deep under anesthetic."

To her, that was the least comfort. She didn't want to cease to feel things. He laughed at her insistence.

She had felt everything so sharply that day. Her perceptions had quickened; she saw through two pairs of eyes. The color of earth and rocks and sky and sea had more vividness than ever before. It was as though the sound of summer wind in the chaparral was new to her ears, and she had to tell Dirk how it sounded in winter. Wind in oak branches is different from wind in pines, and wind rustles brush in another different way. She told him how in stormy weather you could hear the wind coming down the hill— you heard it in the sagebrush and greasewood and sumac bushes above a long time before it reached where you were.

She told him what winter rains did to the hills, how streams loped down the canyons, how wind waves seemed to make a look of foam as they stirred acres of wild grain.

She showed him the brush that would be a purple and blue sea of wild lilac in the spring. It was as though she said, "I give you all this. And there is myself, too."

There was another thing she loved about him. It was his voice. She listened so intently that she learned by heart everything he said that day. She knew all his life now, as far as it had gone.

When they started home at last, down the shadowing hills, she felt a great sense of belonging. Not once had he touched her, yet she felt completely his.

CHAPTER 16 ⌒

But as time went on she realized that part of her happiness was due to a feeling of expectancy, a feeling that the best was yet to come. At times she felt impatient. But she didn't worry; she felt so very sure. She knew that Dirk's restraint was a thing she admired.

Without giving it any thought she had assumed that when she knew a man she could love, he would be the man who would want her. It was incredible that it should be otherwise. To feel this way seemed part of a woman's heritage. She didn't know that she had been led to believe this through things she had heard and read all her life.

She was surprised when realization came to her slowly. Obviously Dirk was fond of her companionship, but he was not in the least in love with her.

At first she thought, what is wrong with him that he doesn't see how exactly right we are for each other? And then she thought the fault must be hers. She looked at her reflection. She was not beautiful, but certainly she was a better-looking woman than he was a man. Something was wrong with her. I'm not feminine enough. Look at my ugly hands. And I'm so tall and straight...

Then she thought, but of course he loves me. He thinks he shouldn't. He thinks I'm better off here, that I would never leave my home. Or maybe he doesn't want to love any woman. He's ambitious. Maybe he loves me and won't give in to it.

She realized how unlike they were in certain ways. He liked her beautiful hill country, but he could be content in a city. But didn't he know that she would leave this land and go away with him, that though she would probably be happiest all her days here, she still wanted to be where he was?

Then she thought reasonably how love is all a matter of gland secretions, anyway. She had seen how rapturously two people could love at first, and how finally love dwindled into nothing but affection. She knew that individuals change constantly.

Again she thought, why doesn't he know how it should be? Modern women aren't shy and hesitant. At least we say that. But there's pride. You can't just go and tell a man how you feel. Dirk was kind. If he didn't love her he might be embarrassed for her sake. He might pity her. She thought with amusement of girls in Victorian novels, girls all tremulous like herself, waiting for the man to declare himself. She had never imagined being in such a situation. She didn't know how to cope with it.

Still, until the time of his leaving for the east she had hope. She watched for a certain expression on his face, listened for a word that wasn't spoken.

When he left she only said, "Send me a postcard sometime."

But she still hoped. She hoped for a letter in which Dirk would write everything that had been left unsaid. Every day she vowed she wouldn't go to the post office, and every day she went.

No letter came. Sometimes she felt anger at Dirk. More often she was angry with herself.

She told herself that she could get over being in love the same way she could get over having a cold in her head. It was all a matter of time.

Things went on as usual. Every day she did the same things. Animals had to be looked after; a day had so many hours and so many tasks.

CHAPTER 17 ✑

Sometimes the girl wondered what was going to happen to her. She loved her house and her mother and father. She loved the big barn and the land and the animals. Her love was like a nest holding all the things she knew, and she belonged in the nest, for she loved herself and her own way of living.

If she lived at home and never married she would watch her mother and father grow old and die. Perhaps while she was still young they would leave her. She didn't think they were strong. Last summer's heat had sickened her father and she had been doing most of the work. All summer her mother had looked tired and worried. If anything happened to these two people, and if Dirk never returned, she couldn't think what she would do.

It was remarkable the way people managed to live on when they seemed to have lost everything they loved. Mothers whose children had died, children whose parents had died, men who had lost every penny they earned. When the end of one way of living came, some new way began. People just didn't fall down and die when everything was lost.

When a calf was butchered the cow grieved and wouldn't eat and wouldn't let down milk. Just when you thought she couldn't endure living any longer she seemed to brighten up and forget her grief. It went the same way with people.

Some folks said they got along because they trusted in the Lord. It was good they felt that way. Humans and animals had to have the feel of a refuge somewhere. Animals endured misery because they couldn't help it. Cows didn't look very far back and certainly never thought far ahead. Yet the girl felt as though they depended on the earth itself for comfort. It was hard to make her thoughts clear about this. But it seemed as if every beast had a secret retreat somewhere. When animals sickened they withdrew into themselves. Sometimes it seemed that an old cow or horse simply made up its mind to die, as a caged bird will do.

Sometimes the girl could draw power from the earth. Sometimes it seemed as though fields and hills and sky were brooding over her—as though the earth itself were a beating heart.

Once, when a cow was having trouble bearing a calf, the girl and her father worked until they were weary. The girl could stand it no longer. She ran away from the suffering animal and flung herself face down on the sun-warmed earth. She couldn't call on Heaven for help; it was too remote. It was the earth that fed and rested its creatures, and it was to the earth that the girl appealed. Her body and her mind demanded, implored. She stretched out in an agony of appeal. All the great strength that caused seeds to burst and push life toward the sunshine, all the energy that moved the earth to the sun and away, that kept stars in line and brightened and darkened the moon—all of everything, mountains, stars, seas—must lend their strength. With all her body and mind she willed the animal's recovery. Sweat chilled her brow, her clenched hands were wet. Her heart pounded and then beat softer. The land fell quiet as she relaxed in desperation. Her fingers spread out limply. She felt light as a winged seed, as small as an ant. But still her mind kept begging the earth for help.

After a space of time she became aware of someone calling her name. She stood up. "I'm coming," she answered her father, and hurried back to the cow.

The calf was on the ground, gasping to live. The cow was resting.

The girl trembled with a feeling of gratitude. It seemed as if the earth had listened.

But she couldn't know if the earth would always be her friend. She found comfort in the hills when creatures she loved had been sold or had died. But it might be that someday she would look with reproach at sunshine because it lighted the hills tenderly, as if there were no such thing as death. It might be a hurt to hear lovemaking birds, or watch squirrels frisking on the rocks.

CHAPTER 18 ⌐

Horses took great pleasure in rolling on the earth. Once the girl had had a pet lamb that would get down and roll like a horse. Cows didn't ever take a comforting roll to rub itchy spots or brush off flies, but if you wanted to see a herd of cattle suddenly become calfish, just turn them loose on a freshly plowed field. The springy feel of it between their cloven hoofs, or the smell of it, or maybe just the look of it seemed to drive them quite out of their wits. They would run with lowered heads, kick their heels high, spin themselves around, and engage in pushing contests with one another. They would bellow and leave their mouths open, and strings of frothy saliva would drip as if the very earth made their mouths water. Old heavy-uddered cows would cavort as foolishly as their youngest calves; old bulls would roar until you thought of thunder over the mountains.

Young heifers would try to bellow like their fathers. Soft bare earth made tomboys of them all.

One fall day when Joseph was not yet a year old, the girl was late getting home to do evening chores. She was cross to find that the cows had pushed a gate down, and horses and cattle were scattered all over the neighborhood.

Most of the cows were grazing along the road, and the horses had to be chased from a neighbor's garden. When she got everyone home she saw that young Joseph was not with them.

Then she heard a deep rumble that cracked embarrassingly into a calfish blat, and there was little Joseph in the newly planted oat field. On Pete she started after him. Joseph saw her coming and made what he planned to be most threatening sounds. But his voice would crack, like that of a boy who tries to speak like a man. Still he did his best to be a bull; he made the soft earth fly over his shoulder. Seeing that even this didn't scare Pete, he nearly stood on his head. He buried his little horns in the earth and rubbed earth all over his head and face and then spun around and frolicked across the field. He seemed to bounce higher after every touching of hoofs to earth.

Pete tore after him, turning this way and that to head him back, but Joseph would whirl and go charging in a different direction. At first the girl was cross at wasting so much time—she was late enough anyway, and darkness was coming fast. She made Pete stop to rest and then she began to laugh because the antics of the little bull were growing sillier all the time.

He stopped running, put his head low, held his front legs stiff and pivoted around, his rear end whirling dizzily, his tail sailing high. And thinking himself very fine, he made the most anguished sounds he could command.

But for all his playing he was truly enraptured with the earth. He was in ecstasies of delight. Being a little bull, he couldn't write a poem or sing a song, and the need to express himself was very great. So, until dark, he praised the earth with all the exuberance of his stocky young body. And when he was tired at last it seemed that he might well have gathered a lot of the goodness of the earth into his very bones.

CHAPTER 19 ✎

The girl was thinking about growing old. She had stopped by to see the Weavers the last time she went for the mail. They lived with their married son and his family on the edge of town. Their daughter-in-law was an unpleasant woman.

But Grandpa Weaver was happy. He had a hobby.

People saved newspapers for him and he read all the death notices. Grandpa was a Native Son. He remembered when the city by the coast was a small country town. Grandpa knew scores of old men, some in the city, some living in the back country. Now it gave Grandpa a kind of pleasure to see his friends' names in print. He cut out their funeral announcements and pasted them neatly in a little black book. Sometimes he grumbled because for weeks he wouldn't find a familiar name. Then maybe he would see two in the same column.

He showed the girl his latest find. "Why I knew him," he gloated, "when he didn't have one dime to jingle against another. Borrowed money to start in the grocery business. He'd take one cracker out of a sack to keep it from weighing a fraction too much. He was honest but close. Mighty close. But he done all right." Grandpa sighed with satisfaction. "Well, he's gone. And here I be."

Grandpa was the dry leaf that held fast to the shivering tree. And when other leaves dropped Grandpa held on tighter. But he couldn't cling forever.

The girl wondered why Grandpa held on so stubbornly. His son's wife was forever scolding him.

But Grandpa liked his tobacco and he liked to sit in the sun. He had his death notices to pore over.

She wondered if the son would remember to paste Grandpa's funeral notice in the little black book.

His wife didn't share her husband's interest. She couldn't have read the obituaries, anyway, because her eyes were failing. She couldn't enjoy talking about the newly dead because she was growing deaf.

But her hands were good; her fingers were as supple as they'd ever been. Grandma Weaver knitted. When she ran out of yarn she ripped something up and started over again. She knitted all day long and half the night. She got along with little sleep.

She wanted the girl to learn to knit. "It's something to learn when you're young. An old woman can't learn. It's so nice to do when you can't do anything else. Imagine if I couldn't knit. I can't see nor hear good. I can't get around much. When you grow old you'll be glad to have something useful to keep you busy. Young folks never seem to plan on growing old."

No, the girl thought, she never had planned on growing old. Death seemed almost easier to imagine than old age. She never had thought that the time might come when she'd wish for some way of amusing herself. When you were young life gave you a number of things. Then it began taking them away. Life was an Indian giver. Some day there was only one thing left. You could sit and knit or you could cut out death notices. Eventually you wouldn't have that much. You still had death. One thing more to do.

Some day she might forget the sound of music, fail to hear human voices. Printed pages would be black and white blurs. Her fingers might grow stiff, and curved like roots, so she couldn't knit if she wanted to.

She felt cold in the sunshine.

She thought, "I can drowse like old Juno and dream. I'll dream over all the things I've ever thought or done."

But she thought maybe she'd be like a thin old horse, an old horse that doesn't know he is old, only feels that he is tired and miserable.

CHAPTER 20 ∽

Her feeling toward death was more of hatred than of fear. She had seen a great deal of death. She had seen a great deal of birth and she couldn't deny that birth was a beginning of pain and trouble, and death an ending of all discomfort. Still she hated death, for while the dead are past suffering, they are, as she had told Dirk, also done with pleasure. No sun can ever warm them, no sound shake them with delight.

She wished she could believe, as some people did, that the clear sweet call of a silver trumpet would command the dead to arise: multitudes of people rising from the earth; the world so thronged there would be no room to step; everything that had ever lived and died called back to life. Would they come gladly, or would they stir, like sleepers half awake, and then turn to darkness again?

Her thoughts pushed further. Let all flowers blossom into resurrection. Fancy the garden of the world if every flower that had ever bloomed should bloom again!

And animals. Let all the little calves come trooping back to her. The calves that she had watched fatten so that they might die. Would they forgive her for loving them and then selling their bodies for meat?

That was a trouble. She who hated death accepted death as a business partner. Life, death and herself, they worked together. They worked with a calf dealer who brought three-day-old calves from dairies and left them with her until they were fat. Then he brought more new ones when he came to take the fattened ones. So at the same time she sorrowed for the plump calves that were leaving, her heart warmed toward the small ones that would be hers for a while. She fed them carefully, dosed them when they were sick, saw that they had sunshine and shelter, and loved them well. The dealer said she raised the best calves of anyone. She didn't tell him it was because calves thrive on loving care. She never gave a name to any of the calves she kept for a little while. Once name an animal and it is twice as hard to sell. Their personalities are too strong anyway, they are human enough without wearing human names.

Once she had a dream she couldn't forget. She saw a long line of childlike creatures. She saw them vaguely in her dream. They weren't animals and they weren't children. But they seemed to be the embodied personalities of all doomed calves and lambs. They were being herded toward death and they cried dumbly to be saved. And while she wanted to save them she herself was helping drive them.

She kept trying to tell them that she couldn't help them, that it had to be. And they kept asking, strangely without sound, "Why? Why?"

She reasoned that if she didn't fatten and sell these calves someone else would. And their short lives might not be as happy in someone else's care. So whether she sold them herself or not they were doomed.

Looking at her grazing cows, she thought that the ones who would die natural deaths would die in more agony than those that were killed quickly for beef. Yet she would hurry away from the scene of a butchering, while she would do anything possible to comfort an animal dying of sickness.

She thought of her travels on horseback in the hills back of her father's land. She had followed trails so dim that they dwindled into little paths rabbits used. It was lonely country and she loved it; the loneliness made her feel hidden and safe. In canyons and small hidden valleys trees grew—live oaks, sycamores, willows and cottonwoods. The rest of the land was given over to chaparral.

She might feel she was in a place where man had not been, and then she would see on a hill, or in a small valley, tall eucalyptus trees in a row. The trees said that here man had been. The native trees had planted themselves, but the tall trees had been set out by the hand of man. Near them the girl might come across all that was left of a barn or a house, perhaps just a foundation, or roofless walls. The feeling of death and desolation hung about these abandoned homesteads. Yet it was not a depressing feeling, here with the quiet kind hills all about.

Where man had been, man's animals had been also. In a clump of brush, or in the shelter of a narrow draw, or maybe on a hill's slope the girl would find bones of those that had known these hills before her. Skulls of cattle, eyes no longer empty, but filled with grass, or encircling the stem of a plant. Wild cucumber vines curling around white horns. Grass separating the vertebrae. She never found a skeleton complete; hungry coyotes and wildcats had long ago scattered the parts. Sometimes all to be found were skull and horns.

Near horse bones she usually found little curved shells of hoofs, no frog or quick left. Dried rinds that had once been colt hoofs were now shrunken to the hoof size of a new foal.

The girl thought it strange that these signs of death did not seem bad. The ivory whiteness of these bones made her think that death treated them better than it did the buried bones of men who had owned the cattle. Out here the decaying flesh was soon cleaned off by animals, air and small forms of life. Under the earth dissolution must be a longer and more hideous process. Here at last the bones were free of the flesh that kept them from wind and sun. But the poor bones of man were ever in darkness. She wished that her own bones, when she was done using them, could rest cleanly in the sunshine.

CHAPTER 21 ⤴

Seeing Beckie's father drive past one morning made the girl think of Beckie. She hadn't thought of Beckie for years. She wondered if Beckie's family thought of her any more. Beckie's family had done a lot of marrying since Beckie had died. Her brothers and sisters had married, her mother and father had divorced each other and married new mates. Beckie would now have a stepmother and a stepfather and a real mother and a real father and sisters-in-law and brothers-in-law and nieces and nephews. Besides that she would probably have several children of her own.

Now there probably wasn't anything left of Beckie but her bones. Seven years is a long time for a girl like Beckie to be dead. She had been dead almost half as many years as she had been alive. You could imagine pale dreamy girls who might be the dying sort. But Beckie was round and rosy and her mind was always concerned with her body. Deprived of a body, how could there be the slightest ghost of Beckie? Putting clothes on her body, keeping her cheeks and lips rouged and her hair curled was Beckie's life work. As soon as she was physically adult only one thing interested her. She called it love.

She was so obviously and innocently passionate that the boys teased her. A masculine arm thrown carelessly over her shoulder was an excitement to her. She fell in love with every man she danced with. Her body surged with life, her eyes were always liquid bright, her breath came quickly, blushes mixed with rouge on her cheeks.

But what kept her so aglow with life was what eventually betrayed her.

The girl would always remember Beckie's face as she had seen it in a mirror. It was at a party. They had stood before a bedroom dresser, smoothing hair, powdering noses. And Beckie had talked, seeking her own eyes in the mirror, not the girl's. She didn't look at her own face critically as most girls do before a glass. She patted her face and hair lovingly, turned her head this side and that, unconscious of her vanity, pleased with her warm body.

The girl remembered thinking, "She adores herself. And she's not pretty, really. Her face is too big, her teeth crowd her mouth. Why, I'm better looking!"

That was the last time she ever saw Beckie. A good thing that no one can glimpse the future. What if Beckie had seen a death's head mocking her reflection? It had been there all the time, grinning over Beckie's round shoulder, but it had been invisible.

Soon after that Beckie, at sixteen, was married. Six months after her wedding day she was dead. Before she died she said she hoped her baby would live. They didn't tell her it had died.

After seven years, when you thought about it, it still seemed strange that Beckie was dead. In seven years Beckie had missed so much of the things she had loved. Not sunshine or sweet air, but dancing the big apple, contests of jitterbugs, swing music, and the funny hats girls wore now.

It was sad to think that Beckie had been deprived of living simply because life had surged so strongly in her body.

CHAPTER 22 ⌒

Sometimes there was such a quietness on the land that each small sound stood distinct and alone. If a bird chirped it was as if the only bird in the world made the only sound that it could. Before night came on the stillness was breathless and the hills grew intensely bright.

Everybody was wishing for rain; this long dry fall was getting on people's nerves. If the girl kept on, following the cows further every day, all the roadside grass would be grazed off. But she didn't worry. It seemed as if the unchanging days, the ever clear sky, the yellowing leaves and the dry grass had made her feel so quiet and contented that it was no use to fret about anything.

Morning after morning she saw the mountains clear with color, and she didn't tire of watching them. In the intense heat and dryness of midmorning she sat in cold shade and looked and listened to small happenings around her. Birds and ground squirrels and insects in the grass held her attention. The laws of design entranced her. The gods had taken such care and pains over the decoration of a small insect wing that the girl could feel that nothing was too trifling to be overlooked.

When she thought about how each small life feels itself the center of the universe—how sunshine, rain or food is good or bad, depending on each individual need, how certain times and conditions cause different meanings for each thing that lives—she was overwhelmed with wonder and despair at the way the world ends a thousand times a minute. If she crushed an insect the sun was blotted out, the stars fallen, the earth shattered—forever and ever the universe ceased to be for one atom of living.

Then she thought, for every time a particle of life broke out of an egg, crept from a cocoon, or pushed out of a womb, the pageantry of earth and sun, moon and stars, color and sound and scent and feeling was created again.

People were forever inquiring about the purpose of life and speaking of the great riddle of creation. As far as the girl could see life was its own excuse for being. Life was given to be lived. The tiniest insect served its purpose if it grew to its utmost in its hour in the sunlight. It seemed that everything was busy growing, and, barring accident, a thing didn't start dying until it had stopped growing. That might be the secret of the redwood trees up north. It is said that not one of those trees ever died a natural death. For thousands of years they had been growing, and they must keep growing to keep living.

Humans stopped growing too soon. They became adults and settled into a dull way of living and thinking, and minds and bodies began decaying together. The girl thought that for herself this was good growing weather. No pasture grass was growing these November days, but while she was waiting for the time of grass she could be growing inwardly.

This job of watching grazing cattle took her thoughts far. It made her think of shepherds and herdsmen in ancient times and lonely places. Before Bible times people were watching grazing beasts and thinking thoughts not unlike her own. A boy named David had watched sheep and thought, "That old ewe looks pretty good," or "That big ram will bear watching, he might get mean." Just as the girl thought, "Old Whitey doesn't look bad," or "Joseph might turn on me some day, for all his gentleness now."

Many people were her kinsmen. Now in different places all over the world people were watching grazing herds. Somewhere on the night side of the earth a boy might be guarding his flock and looking at those clock stars around the North Star. Nearer home, over in New Mexico, perhaps, a Navajo girl was in the sunshine watching sheep.

CHAPTER 23 ～

One morning the girl was drowsy. Because early mornings
were cold and midmornings were hot she sometimes grew
sleepy, the way a person grows sleepy coming into a warm
room out of the cold.

A woodpecker kept up a steady rhythm of pounding
and a wild dove was making the same sad sound, over and
over. The girl curled up on a bed of fallen sycamore leaves
and the next minute she was asleep.

But she didn't sleep long. Something was blowing on
her face; something was moving her hair. She opened her
eyes to stare into the anxious face of the old white cow.

Whitey blew a troubled breath and lowed with
almost the same moaning sound she made each year when
she spoke to her new calf. The girl sat up and Whitey was
reassured. She bent her head to be scratched between her
crooked horns. It pleased her when someone troubled to

dig the ticks out of her ears, and she liked to be rubbed under her chin where hide hung loose and itching.

In her white face her eyes looked bigger and blacker than the eyes of other cows. There was no end to their depth. They were neither sad nor happy. They were just two organs of vision from which an old cow looked at the world. Once a year they brightened when they looked at the new calf. Whitey had beautiful calves. She had borne over a dozen of them. By now she was more than a great-grandmother; she was an ancestor. For years the girl had been hoping that Whitey would have a pure white bull. So far all her calves had had dark markings.

She said to Whitey, "Next time, see that you have that white bull. Then you can be a retired matron."

Whitey seemed to consider. The girl said, "But now get busy and graze."

Whitey needed to work harder at grazing than younger cows because she had lost two important teeth. A cow needs all her lower front teeth to help her toothless front upper jaw and her tongue gather grass. You might say that every time old Whitey reached for six straws of grass she gathered only one.

Whitey was like an ancient family retainer. It was hard to remember when she hadn't been on the place. She was going to stay until she grew so old and sick she'd have to be shot. Whitey was one old cow that was never going to market. The girl wished she could be as sure about the others.

Animals had nearly all the faults humans had, but they didn't pretend to be better than they were. Some of their human ways were amusing.

Cows and horses adhered as strictly to a rule of precedence as people did in diplomatic circles. Among her cows it was Whitey who had first place at the watering trough or the salt lick. Any one of the big heifers could push her out of the way, but it was never done. It wasn't all a matter of age, either. Among the younger ones it was those that already had calved who took precedence over the less experienced.

In the herd there was one undersized heifer who got herself bred when she was so young that she calved when she was a yearling. Calving before she had her growth caused her to be stunted; she would always be a puny little creature. Yet she carried herself with pride, and when the cattle were crowded together on the road going home, not one of the strong heifers dared jostle the smallest cow. If one tried to crowd ahead of her she shook her short horns so threateningly that the other stepped back. It was as though the little cow knew her own social position and would let no lesser one forget it.

Among the hill horses there was always one who drank first at the spring, and one who must wait patiently while all the others drank, while they rinsed out their mouths, and dozed standing over the water. And the one who waited might be the largest and strongest in the herd, while the first might be old and weak, or young and nimble. It seemed to be a matter of spirit more than strength. But certain it was that there were set rules and regulations.

Among some beasts it seemed that the strongest became the leader. Among wild horses it is said that stallions fight for the leadership of the band. But from what the girl had seen of herds of horses in pasture she was quite

certain that it was some wise old mare who was acknowl-
edged leader. In times of danger it might be the stallion
who struck out ahead. But that could easily be because he
was swiftest. Mares heavy with foal or mares with colts by
their sides naturally would not run so fast.

The girl wondered how animals learned the things
they knew. Sometimes it was as though the earth spoke to
them, as if cows gathered wisdom with mouthfuls of grass.
How else could you account for instinct? It was much surer
than reason.

She would like to know just how much an animal
understood about birth and death. She always showed
Joseph his sons and daughters and he would look with
interest at the newborn and put down his great head to
snuff at it.

The gentlest horse would shy from the scent of death.

She had always wondered what had gone on in the
mind of a black cow who had stood and watched them
bury her dead calf. Late one summer the calf had sickened.
The girl dosed it with every remedy she could think of:
scorched flour, coffee, castor oil, raw eggs and boiled milk.
But it kept on scouring and growing weaker and weaker. It
got so that when she held it up to nurse its mother, it only
licked listlessly at a teat instead of curling its tongue around
it and sucking. She tried to feed it milk from a spoon, but
it wouldn't swallow.

The girl wanted the cow to see it when it was dead, so
she wouldn't go around hunting for it, thinking it had been
taken away. They dragged the calf out to where they were
going to dig the grave and the mother came and stood over

it. She looked at it anxiously and licked it awhile and then turned away, wandering off with the other cows.

But soon she came back again and stood looking at the calf and watching the girl and her father digging in the hard earth. The weather was very hot and they hurried to dig the grave.

All the time they were digging the cow stood there. Once in a while she nosed the calf, and spoke to it, making a soft moaning sound. But most of the time she just stood motionless, not even chewing her cud. She was a sad black shadow in the bright sunshine.

It took several hours to dig the grave deep enough, the earth was so dry. They poured water in the excavation, but it only made hard clay. All the time the cow stood waiting, not seeming to expect anything, but just waiting.

When they rolled the calf into the grave its mother took a quick step forward. She stopped, bewildered, and made a strange roaring sound. She watched earth being thrown over the calf that her body had once held warmly. She wandered around and after a while settled down with the other cows.

But when it came time for evening milking she missed the calf she should have fed. She would not let down her milk for the girl. She stood uneasily in the stanchion. When she was turned out she nosed around the grave and began calling for the calf. All night long she grieved until by morning her voice was hoarse. She made sounds like sobs. She knew that her calf was gone, that she would never see it again.

The girl couldn't comfort the cow as she comforted herself. She couldn't make the cow understand that maybe it was happier for the calf to go before it knew too much about the world. All it had ever known was warm sunshine and kind hands and a mother cow that loved it.

CHAPTER 24 ☜

When the cattle had grazed their way down the road beyond Lost Horse Canyon the girl was reminded of old Ezra. Set back from the road was a sagging henhouse, and that had been Ezra's home. No one knew his last name, or much about him. For a long time he lived in the henhouse and people were so used to him that no one was curious.

Because of his age and poverty the state gave him a small pension every month. For Ezra it was a great deal of money because his needs were few. He went to bed at dark so he didn't have to buy oil for a lamp, he wore clothes people gave him, he didn't believe in eating very much. Aside from feeding himself his only expense was gasoline for his wobbly car. It didn't need much, for the only work it did was to take Ezra to town once a week. Ezra worried about having so much money.

He didn't even have to feed his cats, for the old henhouse was the home of more rats than the cats could eat or scare away. As a matter of fact, the cats and the rats had almost a truce, for when the cats weren't hungry they were too lazy to bother the rats. A narrow ledge, about as high as a man's shoulder, ran all the way around the inside of the henhouse and when darkness came the rats frolicked there, with much fighting and squeaking and mating. When Ezra wasn't sleepy he liked to throw things at the rats from his cot. He kept a pile of stones within handy reach. Sometimes in the darkness he would knock down a rat. He had a place on the wall where he kept score of the number of rats he had hit. It was his only entertainment. As far as he was concerned, the rats were an asset to his dwelling, and he wouldn't have them exterminated. He merely tried to keep down the population to reasonable numbers. In this the cats aided him, though sometimes he worried a little over the growing cat population.

It had been many years since old Ezra occupied the henhouse, but the girl remembered him well. She could remember exactly how he looked, always needing a shave and a haircut. She remembered his bright blue eyes and the kind way he smiled and spoke. Ezra didn't like many people, but when the girl was little he took a fancy to her and always came out to talk when she went by. Sometimes he spoke poetry to her, not very good poetry, but anything that rhymed was poetry to Ezra. Also he took great comfort in his Bible but not in the usual way. He thoroughly enjoyed studying it to find faults and contradictions, and he liked to have a listener when he expounded his theories on the fallacy of religion. He acted as if he were the first one to discover that the world wasn't built in seven days, that two of every kind of animal couldn't find room in Noah's Ark, that no man could be swallowed by a big fish and live to tell folks his adventures.

The day the girl was eleven years old she rode by Ezra's house with a new bridle on Pete, who wasn't old Pete then. When Ezra admired the bridle she told him it was a birthday present, and then Ezra said he would give her a present, too. "It's not ready yet, though. Now if you was to ride by just a bit before dark it'd be ready."

It was September and darkness was beginning to come earlier, but it seemed a long day of waiting. She couldn't imagine what old Ezra had for her. It was a long time before the sun set and shadows folded the hills. Then she jumped on Pete bareback and pounded down the road.

Ezra was waiting for her. "Got here just in time, now look." He pointed to the west. Above a line of apricot color the first star was shining gold. "That star I give to you. My mother gave it to me when I was ten years old, and I've kept it careful ever since. Now it's yours."

At first she felt disappointed. Her idea of a present had been something done up in tissue paper, waiting to be unwrapped. But she wouldn't hurt the old man's feelings so she thanked him politely. He said, "The North Star might be a more useful one to own, but I always liked this one better. It's prettier, and it shows at a nice time of day."

She looked at it and agreed. It surely was a beautiful star. And now it did seem her very own, and a most remarkable sort of present. No one could take it away from her.

The old man cleared his throat. "My mother gave me a lot of presents before she died. Some I kept. That's the very best of the lot."

She thanked him all over again. It certainly was a tremendous thing to be given a star.

Ezra's presents were none of them store presents, for his mother and father never had any money to spend. They lived way back in the hills and ran a few sheep, and once he got a real live lamb for his birthday. It was a twin, and its mother wouldn't care for two lambs. "Drank milk out of a bottle with a rag tied over it, and follered me everywhere, smart as a dog."

"What happened to it?" the girl wanted to know. She hoped it was one of the presents Ezra had kept. But he disremembered. "Likely it grew up and joined the flock."

But another present he kept a long time, he suspected he still owned it, would like to go back sometime and see. It was a sumac bush. Just like a million others. Only his mother gave it to him for Christmas. Since it was his he looked at it more and got a lot of pleasure out of it. Saw what birds came to it, and watched a pair of linnets nest in it. Their nest was lined all soft with shreds of wool they had picked off of bushes and fence wires.

While Ezra stood talking by his door it grew very dark inside. The rats began racing around and when they made too much noise he shouted at them to shut up, as if they were dogs. When they didn't obey him he picked up what he called a clinker and threw it into the darkness. It banged against the wall and for a while the rats subsided into an abashed silence.

"In the morning," said Ezra, "I'll see if I got one."

The coming on of night excited Ezra's cats. They crouched in the dry grass and jerked their tails, and sprang at one another. There were old cats and kittens and half-grown cats, and more and more of them appeared until all around the place were pouncing animals. But not even the softest kitten would let itself be touched when the girl bent to pet one.

So many cats seemed almost evil, and their mad playing seemed more grim than frolicsome. Ezra explained, "It's night that makes 'em so wild. In the sunshine they're nice soft pussy cats, but at dark they grow fierce. I don't bother with 'em at night. Soon as it gets dark they turn into wild animals. I kind of like a cat for being two kinds of animal. There's no variety to a dog."

The girl looked up and saw that her star had set so she thanked Ezra again and said she had better go home. Ever afterward the evening star reminded her of cats and rats as well as of Ezra.

CHAPTER 25 ⁀

It was surely going to rain! Such a dampness was in the air that the girl sat hugging herself and shivering. She didn't like to be cold. But that didn't matter. It was exciting to see the sky dark with clouds. For months, it seemed, every day had been just like the last one. Cold and clear every morning, hot and dry every noon. Now there was such a difference that the blackbirds were whistling to say that rain was coming and they were glad. Blackbirds in swarms, rising and settling among bare branches. Blackbirds thick as flies around spilled milk. Some all dark, some with red flashes on their wings, all of them calling bell-clear and rising in red and black surges.

Besides the sign of blackbirds there was a south wind blowing. Rains came on south winds. The girl remembered reading what one of the mission fathers had said in early California days. He had been asked to pray for rain. He said he would pray, but not until the wind was in the south and blackbirds whistled.

The cows felt the excitement of rain in the air. They brushed their sides on bushes and kicked up their heels. Joseph, the bull, rumbled joyfully. The filly, Flaxie, couldn't settle down to graze. She nipped at Pete and teased him to play with her. He grazed with the air of having one eye on the weather, as if he knew that he had better get a full belly of dry grass. He had shivered in too many rains. The colt, of course, couldn't remember what rain was like.

The clouds looked cumbersome, not as if they found it fun to scud across the sky. But for all their solid look the wind blew them around so that at times there would be flashes of brilliant sunshine.

The girl watched a yellow cottonwood tree. In the movement of sunshine and shadow it looked as though the tree were wired with electricity. The tree would be lighted, and suddenly the light would go out. After seeing the tree brightened, the contrast of shadow on it was so great that for just an instant the tree seemed to have disappeared. For a breath it wasn't there, and then she saw it dully. For a time it stood in shade and then it seemed as if she could almost hear the click of a light switch. The brightness came in a flash and the tree trembled with light, and it seemed that the light came from within it.

If she looked at earth and sky and other trees and rocks and cows and shaded mountains, the magic of the tree's brightening and darkening was not so apparent. But if she looked at no other thing but that one tree standing alone, it was one of the most exciting things she had ever seen done by sun and shade. She watched the tree as though it was the only tree ever grown on earth, and mysteriously the tree continued to turn its light off and on.

Shivering in the damp south wind the girl thought with intense delight that being a living thing should be enough to gladden all beings on earth. She thought that if her body should become injured so that she had always to lie abed, she would still rejoice to be living.

The pleasure she was getting out of this day was a pleasure shared by everyone in the valley. Weather is very important to people who live on the land; city people can understand little about the drama of weather conditions. This day of clouds and wind was a day to bring hope to the dreariest farmer.

A few cars passed and the drivers looked cheerful. One neighbor stopped and shouted heartily, "When are you going to let it rain?"

"Tonight," the girl answered, knowing how the first rain would fall at the end of a day like this. "Tonight it will start sprinkling, and it will keep raining harder and harder, and you'll find mud puddles in the road in the morning."

"Good girl," he beamed, as though the girl really were responsible for the weather's change. "I'm going in and buy me some oat seed right now."

The light went out of the tree and didn't come on again. On a hill across the valley there were still pockets of sunlight but after a while shadows fell evenly. Everything was gray now; even yellow leaves were dull.

The grayer things got, the better the girl felt. A great deal of her satisfaction with life was due to promise of rain.

November Grass

The land was so dry that seeing rain fall on it would give her the same sort of pleasure that she would get from giving a hungry horse a good feed of hay.

She could imagine the way the earth would smell when rain moistened the dust. Oak leaves and brown grass would be cleaned. The cows' coats would be washed too, and the hair on the end of their tails would fall in soft curls. Now the cows had a dusty smell, but after they were cleaned by rain and dried by wind and sun they would have a fresh smell, earthy and good. A warm smell that would make her think of the kindness of mother cows and the softness of spring calves.

The lives of her cows were much like the life of the hills. In spring when the grass was bright and wildflowers grew on the slopes, the cows' udders began to swell and new calves were dropped in the grass. Summer went quietly, and by fall, dropped seeds were hidden in the dust. Then the cows carried new lives in their wombs, and spring would come to them as it did to the hills. Their lives fitted so well into the rhythm of the seasons that the girl couldn't think of spring without thinking of calf time.

The girl longed for rain while she dreaded the coldness to come. She thought that in a week from now the tiny leaves of new grass would lie pale on the earth. But it would be a long wet cold time before grass would be tall and sweet, ready to turn dry.

Cattle and horses would stand hunched and shivering in the storms. The girl wished that all calves and colts would wait until quiet weather to be born. They should be like young meadowlarks that are hatched when the rains are over. Old Californians like to tell that rain never falls while meadowlarks are nesting. It should never fall on the new colts.

In the spring the mares would be brought down to the lower pasture. Those ready to foal could be shut in the barn when it stormed. But old range mares fretted in comfortable stalls. They felt trapped by walls; they wanted to be in the open where they could see clearly in every direction.

Winter could be dramatic enough, with the barn roof leaking and the river roaring on the other side of the pasture fence. This coming rain meant that a number of things would happen. But after all these dry fall days, and after the winter rains, there was coming a time of fulfillment. The girl would have a personal feeling of victory to see how the cattle pulled through hard weather in good shape.

Now with withered grass and dry leaves all around her the girl sat longing for spring. She wanted it to be time for colts to play in the sunshine and calves to sleep in deep grass.

The first rain would bring that time nearer.

CHAPTER 26 ⌒

But it didn't rain. Sometime in the night the girl opened her eyes to see a brightly starred sky. That south wind had blown the rain on to the next county without letting a single drop fall. She thought sleepily, "The old padre couldn't be certain, after all. South wind and blackbirds can be mistaken."

The sun was as bright as ever when she got the cattle settled to graze in the morning. She wasn't greatly dismayed. She was used to false promises.

An old couple who lived up the road came driving along. It was their day to go to town for mail and supplies. And as was his custom the old man stopped the car to ask the girl how she was getting along.

"All right so far. But is it ever going to rain?" she said anxiously.

"Mister says so," said his wife.

The old man had very bright blue eyes and they twinkled at her. "Now then," he said heartily, "what you worried for? It always has rained, hasn't it? What I say is, it always *has* rained—and it always *will* rain!"

She had heard him say that every year as long as she could remember and, sure enough, he had always been right.

The old man and his wife were good people to think about. It was because they looked forward. If their cow had a bull calf when they wanted a heifer they thought surely she would have a heifer next year. If the old woman set a hen and only a few chicks hatched, she said she would have better luck next setting. If the farrowing sow got confused and ate her pigs the sow herself got eaten, and the couple figured that the sow's sister would do herself proud when her time came.

Then maybe the other sow would have only four piglets when a litter of eight or nine had been counted on. Or maybe she would have a big litter and they wouldn't do well. The old woman would take the weaklings in the house, spoonfeed them, and put them to bed on hot water bottles. The pigs that survived would turn out to be the best pigs ever, and Missus would show them with pride.

There was something about living on the land that made people forever hopeful. Good years were always ahead. These old people knew well enough that the most promising colt might bring the bitterest disappointment, that a rainy season might start out well and end in drought, that the prettiest heifer might not give enough milk to pay for her feed. Yet they kept on breeding their animals and planting their fields.

Probably they couldn't ever, in the years they had left, free their land of mortgage. They would surely never get a better car, the roof of their barn repaired, or the new milk house built. Their children, who lived up north in Los Angeles, couldn't understand. They wanted the old folks to stop working and worrying; they could spend a few comfortable years if they would give up the land and come visit their married children.

"Stubborn," the youngsters called them. But it wasn't that. The girl could understand how they felt. Sometimes she herself thought that so many small tragedies happened on the land that she must be in training for some greater calamity. She thought she couldn't endure it at all if this or that happened, and when it did happen, somehow she endured and went on. She went on toward expected delights and unexpected tragedies.

Now the old people were going about their business, since they knew it would rain sometime. It always had.

It was the old man's hopefulness that kept him forever busy. She never went to call on them when he wasn't busy. His wife would say, "Mister's up fixing to pipe water down from the spring," or, "Mister's working on the north fence." Some folks just seemed to relax when it wasn't time to plow or cultivate or harvest, but Mister kept himself busy all the year round so that every fence, shed, watering trough and gate was shipshape.

One warm spring day the girl had stopped by to find the wife sitting under a shade tree by the kitchen door. "Look," she said proudly, "I've let the little turkeys out for the first time today."

Nine soft foster children were being kept in a neat group by an old red hen.

"That there red hen," said Missus, "is the best mother thing we ever had on the place. Now, if I'd let a turkey hen set, them little turkeys would be wore out by now. A turkey hen will just trot her babies around all day, till their little legs are trembly weak. Now that old hen, look at her. She's just kept her babies around under these shade trees all day. Just back and forth under two trees. She don't let 'em get all hot and tired. Now listen to her. See how she clucks at 'em not to go away."

It was a pleasurable sight, those little turkeys being minded so well by that wise hen. The girl could feel how it pleased the old woman to watch the young brood cared for so it would grow up strong and healthy.

That's how it is with people living on the land. That's why the fickle promise of rain hadn't worried the old man a bit.

CHAPTER 27 ⌢

The people who lived along the little road and the people who lived across the valley all knew one another, and knew a lot about each other's business, although they didn't do much visiting back and forth. There was always too much work to do at home.

When they met each other it was usually at the town at the foot of the valley. About three hundred people lived there. The people who lived out of town were constantly making trips to town for mail and groceries, so it was in the post office or the grocery store that you learned neighborhood news. You might not know that your next-door neighbor was sick until you went to town to buy a sack of chicken feed.

Quite a few Mexicans lived there, and Indians from the reservation were always loafing along Main Street.

The young people hated the town, it seemed so dull. They all wanted to live in the city by the coast.

Once a year the town came to life. That was the Fourth of July, the day of the annual rodeo. A full month ahead of time the town began to go Western. The storekeeper, the postmaster, the blacksmith, the harness man, the barber, the filling station attendants all wore cowboy hats and bright shirts. A day or two before the rodeo tourists began coming. Then the town was bustling, and noisy with firecrackers. In the rodeo corrals frightened animals crowded together, miserable with heat and dust. There was a dance at night at the rodeo grounds. The town loved it. It thought itself very wicked.

After the rodeo the community went to sleep for another year. Things seemed quieter by contrast and the town grew bored with itself. It almost longed for a robbery or a murder. After having been a moving-picture place it was hard to become only a typical Western town. It was sad to see the mountain cowboys walking about in faded Levis, work shirts and unshined boots. Instead of the clatter of hoofs on pavement there was the sound of automobiles. The place was exactly like a thousand others, with a national highway cutting through Main Street.

The girl liked the town better when it was not dressed up for the rodeo. She couldn't enjoy a rodeo because her sympathy was with the bewildered animals. No animal was hurt intentionally, but accidents would happen. She thought that being frightened half to death was just as bad as being hurt.

November Grass

Now in the fall the streets were duller than ever. When rain came the town would brighten up. Now there were no seed oats sold by the feed store, no plowshares sharpened by the blacksmith, no mending for the harness man. But people still had to buy groceries and go for the mail.

CHAPTER 28 ᕫ

Twice a week the girl went to town for mail and supplies. And now that she was spending so many hours with the cattle, she was glad to get away. Two days out of seven she brought the cows home an hour early to make ready for the trip.

If there weren't many things to carry home she put saddlebags on Pete and rode him. It was an exciting journey, making it on horseback.

Pete ate his hay while she ate her lunch. She used brush and currycomb on him. She saddled him, adjusted the saddlebags, slipped a bit in his mouth. Pete always fought a moment before he accepted the bit. He preferred the hackamore. But the bit had silver shanks, it was a beautiful bit and a Christmas gift, and Pete must wear it when he went to town. The Indians used their best bits and headstalls when they rode to town, and the girl would not be outdone by any Indian.

Pete stepped out blithely. He knew where he was going. He knew the girl would buy a bunch of carrots for him. He rather liked the excitement of town. Traffic to spook at, maybe some Indian ponies to stand with at the hitching rail. He pretended to be afraid of Indian smells, though he really enjoyed strange scents.

Pete carried himself very well. He held his tail proudly and his head gallantly. He was a flea-bitten gray, growing lighter every year. He had a long wavy white mane and tail. His eyes were big in his light face, the hollows above them were deep, but he had no idea that he was beginning to look like an old horse.

The colt, Flaxie, ran up and down and whinnied. She wanted to go, too. Flaxie was bright sorrel, with white socks and a flaxen mane and tail. She had a blazed face, one bright blue eye and one soft brown. The girl would be proud the day she rode the beautiful colt.

Flaxie ran toward the fence so fast that it didn't seem possible that she could stop in time. At the last moment she wheeled and dashed back, kicking up her heels, twisting her body like a kitten. Pete took quick short steps; Flaxie made him feel excited. Long after they had gone around the bend in the road they heard Flaxie's whinnying. Pete answered her once, then stretched out his neck and began traveling seriously, in a running walk.

His hoofs sounded pleasant on the planks of the bridge by Coyote Canyon. On the dirt again he scuffed up dust. He couldn't sweat comfortably, the day was too dry.

It was hot in the November sun. Where the road climbed a little the girl looked down on the tops of river trees. It seemed that twice as many yellow leaves had fallen since last time. The sun on the leaves was metallic. The world was altogether too bright and dry. It was depressing when everything wanted rain.

There were more men in town these days, as there was so little work to be done on the land. The men loitered when they went for mail and groceries. At home the women were just as busy as ever. As far as their work was concerned the weather scarcely mattered. But the men could enjoy loafing. They liked to gather at the harness shop or the blacksmith's. They got more haircuts this time of year. It wasn't their fault that no plowing could be done until it rained. They could take their leisure with a clear conscience. Men have more fun than women.

The girl thought that old men in small towns have the best times of anyone. When the men were too old to work their wives still cooked and washed dishes, maybe helped take care of grandchildren. But the old men could sit in the sun by the barber shop, drift over to the black-smith's, or watch the harness man mend a pair of shoes. If they hadn't saved up money the state wouldn't let them starve. An old man in a city might lead a dreary life, but in a small town everyone was his friend and he could always find someone to listen to stories he told of the good old days.

The old men looked at her horse judiciously. They loved to see a horse go down the street. They would com-ment on the horse's looks or action, the way the rider sat the saddle. They would be reminded of horses they had once owned. They would clear their throats. "Had a horse similar to that one time," or "That puts me in mind of the time I..."

The girl got the mail and bought some groceries. She smiled and nodded to people as she walked down the street. Every face was a familiar face. Nearly everyone mentioned the weather. "When is it ever going to rain?" or, "How are the cows doing these days?"

One man said, "I'm not worrying about my heifers in pasture. They'll either make it, or they won't. Got a couple of old cows that maybe won't pull through. But I can't make anything if I feed 'em hay, and I ain't got the time to set by the road with them."

That was the general attitude. No man ever thought that he actually starved an old cow to death. Every fall old horses and cows got down and died, but no one admitted that they were starved. They simply hadn't been able to pull through the bad time, their owners claimed. It was the animals' fault that they didn't make it. If a cow was giving milk, or springing, she was kept up and fed, but a dry animal had to forage for herself. There was a lot of hunger in the hills these days. Once the rains started most ranchers would feel that it paid to put out a little hay each day to tide over until the grass grew tall enough to be nourishing. Between the time of the first rain and the time of good grass was a worse period than before it rained at all. There was nothing then; the dry grass was either rotted or beaten into the mud, and if the cattle weren't helped a little they hardly had a chance.

So for all its bright prettiness the land was a cruel mother this season. Back in the hills deer were growing gaunt as cows, with not much but the tough brush to eat. There couldn't be much nourishment in greasewood and sagebrush. Nature was compensating in one way: the springs were not failing.

The leaves were more dazzling than ever when the girl started home. The sunset was bright on stony mountainsides.

Pete wanted to gallop. He had had a very pleasant time in town. Now he wanted to get home to Flaxie. The girl gave him a free rein and for a hundred yards they sprinted. When Pete began to blow hard she pulled him in. There was no need for speed. In the morning she'd be in a hurry to get the cows out to graze, but now it was nearly night.

Darkness came early these days; it was dusk when she reached the barn. Her mother heard Pete's hoof beats and called out the door, "How'd you get along? Is there any mail?"

It made the girl feel as if she had been on a long and important journey.

CHAPTER 29 ⪻

Next day she had the weekly *News* to read. She opened to the Personals and read:

"Who was seen perched in a cottonwood sappling Thursday afternoon while Mathew's bull was pawing dirt?"

There's nothing like a country newspaper, she thought, and read on:

"Walter Henshaw went out deep-sea fishing on the barge Sunday and reports a good catch. How many fish did you feed, Walt?

"Mrs. Timothy Goodman has been spending a week visiting relatives in the city."

The girl chuckled at that. The *News* might as well have said, "Timothy Goodman was drunk last week." Timothy Goodman could be good only so long, then he became very drunk and his wife left him until she thought he would be sober. One time she stayed away too long and returned to find him on a second spree. Without seeing

Timothy, there were two ways of telling when he was drunk. You knew he was drunk when his wife wasn't home, and you knew he was drunk when the gate to his calf pen was open. When Timothy felt the time had come to drink liquor, the first thing he did was to turn his calves out so they could do the milking.

The town looked like such a simple kindly place that it was hard to believe it wasn't all it seemed. It was known that the minister had told someone that this town was a bad place for growing boys. There was a lot of gossip and many quarrels. It was even rumored that Buddy Runckle had pulled a knife on Robert McCane. That had seemed ridiculous because the girl couldn't fancy any man caring enough about Flossie McCane to stab another for her sake. But some men have the same instincts as bulls and stallions, and jealousy has driven many an animal to fight to the death.

When the girl thought about the town she saw the bad side of its character in a different way from most people. On two occasions only had the town seemed wicked in her eyes.

One hot summer day she was walking slowly along when she looked up to see a woman she disliked coming toward her. Mrs. Fitzgerald was her name and she was an organizer and a manager, liking only those whom she could dominate. Now she began to talk about the girl becoming a member of the junior Woman's Club, and the girl wasn't interested. Clubs were all right for people who lived in town and had nothing else to do, but the girl was too busy with more important things.

She wanted to get away and she kept backing up, but Mrs. Fitzgerald kept moving closer as she talked. The girl began to feel like a small animal about to be eaten by a larger one. There was a horrible fascination about the closeness of Mrs. Fitzgerald's face. At the moment the woman seemed the impersonation of all the petty gossip the town was noted for. The calm part of the girl's mind told the frightened half that it was being unreasonable, but the frightened half kept begging for escape. The girl backed away another step. She backed off the sidewalk, stumbled over the curb, fell into the street.

Mrs. Fitzgerald stared coldly at her. "Well," she said, "I was only trying to shade your eyes with my hat brim." And she went away without putting out a helping hand.

The other time the town hadn't seemed a good place was after a heavy rain. Riding down a back street, the girl was surprised to see a little striped skunk daintily and leisurely sipping water from a clean puddle. The girl stopped her horse to watch the little thing. It was very careful not to get its feet wet, and after it drank it began washing its face with its handlike feet. It utterly ignored everything else in the world. It was a polite little skunk, minding its own business.

Some children came out of a house, stared at the little animal, and shouted. They rushed back into the house, and out came their mother and a bigger boy with a gun.

"Oh," the girl begged, "don't shoot it. It does no harm."

The woman and children grew angry with her. Skunks were bad, they said.

And the little skunk, who meant no harm at all, died as it washed its face. It died for no reason except that it was what it was and it didn't know that the town was a dangerous place in which to stop for a drink of water.

CHAPTER 30 ⌒

But on a summer night the town seemed wholly good. The girl felt very tender toward that little town when a star marked the end of a street after a hot day. The people seemed like refugees from the wilderness. Coyotes howled on the outskirts but only the boldest ventured among streets and houses.

Mothers and fathers, glad that the sun had gone down, sat on porches and talked quietly. Children liked playing outdoors after supper; they weren't so cross and quarrelsome as when the sunshine had been hot. Cows, staked in vacant lots, sighed drowsily, grateful that they were in shade at last.

On a winter night the town was warm with lights, but in summer people liked to leave their houses dark and sit outdoors. The dark streets would have been a good place for lovers to stroll, but instead of walking together the young men and women were hurrying along the highways in cars. The girl wondered if the old-fashioned kind of courtship hadn't been more satisfying.

When she rode along the dim streets and thought of tired men home from work, and women resting after the dishes were washed, and children soon to be put to bed, she felt compassionate toward all the people in the world. Life seemed full of gentleness.

It seemed especially so when she turned Pete down the street called Mexican Alley. There the children were naked in the darkness. Their brown feet scuffed the cooling dust. When someone chorded a guitar and began to sing, the girl held very still to listen. Song on a dark street meant more than the words and music told. It meant plaintiveness and happiness, one a part of the other. Even the liveliest of Mexican songs held a feeling of sorrow.

A song ended in laughter, and silence lasted a little while. Sometimes a song started haltingly and stopped, and a new song was tried. It was as though the singer were seeking for the one song that would say the way he felt, the song most suitable to himself and the street and the warmness of night.

The night was worthy of song. It must be because the dark was good to the shabbiest house and the most untidy street. Anything that might look unsightly in sunshine was not there at night.

The town was a beautiful place, and all its people were gracious and kindly now.

Dirk thought so, too, when he went there with her one summer night.

CHAPTER 31 ⌒

The people that gathered together in the little town were of the usual type, but a different kind of human lived in the lonely hills, the kind of person that was considered queer, like the man named John of the Wilderness.

The girl thought of Wilderness John because now the cows were grazing near Chicken Hawk Canyon, and up the canyon lived John. He was a shy little man who never shaved and never wore shoes. About once a month John walked down to ask for mail and buy a few supplies. No one ever saw him receive a letter, but he always asked for mail.

He did not come alone; always two or three of his goats came with him. They crowded close around him, brown ones and white, and they made tremulous questioning sounds. When they saw a dog they drew so close to John that he could scarcely step, and he touched their heads and spoke soothing words that only the goats could understand. People said that John knew a special language for his goats, and another language for his bees.

People said all sorts of things about John of the Wilderness. They all agreed that he was crazy as a loon. Some said that he had gold buried under his shack. Some said that he loved a wife who had run away, that he still hoped for a letter from her.

Once the girl had made him unhappy. She liked to ride up the canyon and talk to John and look at his goats. Half a hundred of them kept a great space cleared of brush and grass all around John's little house. Some had long white hair, some were brown and looked like deer, some were black and brown and white, some were golden, some were roan like a horse. The whole great herd wanted to follow John wherever he walked, and John and his goats looked like creatures out of a fairy-tale book.

There was always a sound of tinkling bells and bleating kids.

The time she had distressed John was the time she had forgotten to shut Juno up when she started for her ride. The hound marched quietly at Pete's heels, and the girl didn't think anyone would mind.

But when the goats saw Juno they all ran crying for John. Every one of them was terrified and John looked terrified, too. The girl called the dog and rode back down the trail out of sight. There she tied the hound to a tree and went back to assure John that she meant no harm.

She found him talking to his goats as he would talk to frightened children. He called them by name. "Lily Lee,

Rebecca Sue, Nelly Ann…" He loved them so that nearly every one had double names.

"I'm sorry," the girl said, "I'm sure Juno wouldn't harm them."

Wilderness John looked at her reproachfully. His gray beard trembled. He shook his head. "You shouldn't have such an animal. You should have only grass eaters. Sheep, goats, cows, horses. Those are kind creatures. A dog is wicked. A cat is a devil. Now if you get rid of that hound I'll give you a sweet little white kid. She'll follow you and never hurt anything."

"But I couldn't part with Juno. She's old and she needs me."

The girl had never heard John talk so much as he did that day. He spoke quickly and nervously. He twisted his hands. "The meek shall inherit the earth," he said. He was going to live until that day came. Until no deer was ever frightened, no lamb slaughtered. The birds would sing endlessly; never a startled sound would be heard in all the gentle world. Fawns would come out of hiding in the spring and play unafraid in the clearings, leaping in the sunshine like fish rising out of water.

The girl nodded approval to everything he said, until he felt better and better. He felt so good at last that he gave her a cup of goat's milk with honey stirred in it. To him, goat's milk and honey was the finest food in the world. He lived on that and nothing else, and when he offered such a drink to anyone it was the highest compliment he could pay. Drinking goat's milk and honey was like taking communion to him. It was rich and sweet. The girl drank slowly and gratefully, and John watched her ten-derly, as a missionary would watch a converted heathen partake of bread and wine.

"That's better than eating flesh, isn't it?" he said. "You will come again and I will tell you more. But never let me see you up here with that beast."

Without waiting for her answer he walked away, and all the goats pattered after him, up over a rise and down into a dip out of sight.

CHAPTER 32 ⇐

The Indian reservation at the eastern end of the valley was very like the town at the western end. There were no stores, of course, no Main Street or post office, but there were little houses, and the Indians seemed to live very much like other people in a small community. The same types to be found anywhere were found on the reservation, the gossips, the drunkards, the good husbands and bad. The Indian children took the school bus every day, going through grammar grades and high school with the white children.

Most of the Indians had cars and radios and enjoyed going to the movies. The men dressed like ranchers; the younger women dressed like other young women; only the old grandmothers wore long, brightly colored skirts.

The girl was amused whenever she was riding Pete and a car load of Indians passed. They stared at her as if they were about to say to each other "How picturesque and quaint these white natives are!"

Of course the Indians had ponies, but they didn't ride them, or drive a wagon unless a car was not available. What was the use of poking along at a horse's gait, when one could go fast in a machine? So most of the ponies were free in the hills and colts grew up as wild as deer. Sometimes they strayed out of the reservation and bothered ranchers but the Indians hated to trouble to round them up. In the fall ponies grew gaunt, some of them died; in the spring they were fat and colts were born. Anyone who wanted to buy a pony could pay fifteen dollars and then go pick out what he wanted and catch it. If he couldn't get the pony cornered and roped, it was still his horse; the Indian had the money and didn't care. Lots of the uncaught ponies belonged to white men who were never able to claim them.

Once, the reservation land and ponies and cows had been divided equally among the Indians. Now one or two families owned most of the land and stock. Peon games, cards and dice were responsible for this. The Indians loved to gamble and it was not unlawful for them to gamble on the reservation. But the Indian women seemed to have lost all enthusiasm for games of chance. At the fiestas they wouldn't trouble to get behind their men and chant during night-long games. The peon game requires a poker face, and the chanting of women is supposed to confuse the opponents. Now the Indian wives claimed it made them feel silly to get up before white people at fiestas and sway and chant.

With one exception the Indians seemed to have more freedom than the white men. They could gamble all they liked, they could hunt out of season, they had no financial worries. They ought to be satisfied. Instead they were forever complaining because they could not openly buy liquor. Even so, they had all the whisky and wine they could afford to buy. It was said that several men in town made very good livings selling liquor to the Indians.

In the face of all that it might seem that the Indians were ordinary people, and the girl would have thought them very dull except for one thing.

That was their graveyard. The dead were buried around the adobe chapel, and the chapel and the graveyard were the only reminders that the Indians were primitive people, after all. The girl never rode through the reservation without stopping at the chapel and walking among the graves. The chill of the chapel was enough to remind the Indians of the inevitableness of death. It was sunless and dusty, and the holy pictures on the walls were badly colored prints. The chapel door was always open, so anyone who wished could go in and pray. But the girl had never seen an Indian at prayer or a candle burning. Apparently no one loved that place enough to keep flowers by the Virgin's image, or to wipe the dust out of her staring eyes. For all they had been taught, the Indians seemed to find little comfort in their church. To some people there is a symbolic connection between the place of worship and the beloved dead. The Indians must have felt they had honored the church enough when they buried their dead so near it.

It was not to the church that they turned in sorrow, but to the land their dead lay under.

There they toiled lovingly, decorating crosses with paper flowers. In the spring wildflowers were too common to be good enough for dead people. In the summer there were no wildflowers. Anyway, paper flowers did not fade with the swiftness of real flowers. So they put paper and bits of colored ribbon on the graves.

Many graves had no formal markers. To these the Indians gave small treasures. They placed colored saucers in the earth, and in the saucers they put little toy rabbits such as children play with at Easter.

It was those pathetic rabbits, weatherworn and tired looking, that told more about the Indians than their half-forgotten chants and all their love of modern ways. The paper flowers above the dead spoke truly of the simple minds and hearts of these primitive people.

CHAPTER 33 ✎

The girl would be thinking of other things and then the thought of Dirk would come into her mind. She didn't want to think of him very much, and yet she would keep remembering, or seeing something that made her wish for Dirk to see it, too.

Sometimes she could think about him quietly, and other times the thought of him tormented her.

She could go quite a long time without allowing herself to remember him at all. Then there he would be, so clear in her mind that she wondered if maybe he wasn't thinking of her, too.

At such times she couldn't understand why there was no word from him. After all, they were good friends. It seemed strange that he could be too busy or too forgetful to send some kind of letter.

His letter might have been lost somehow. He would be wondering why she didn't answer.

While her cattle grazed the girl thought out what kind of letter she should write. Casual, but not too casual. She would say that November was beautiful, though the land needed rain. She would tell him how she was saving hay by letting the cows eat roadside grass. She would add I think of you often, and all the happy summer days.

But I've got lots of other things to think about, she told herself. I needn't let myself think of him. The world is crowded with people, and things are happening all the time, even to the few I know. I needn't be wondering about what's happening to Dirk.

Her mind wasn't always obedient. It went right on composing another letter to Dirk. It was a waste of time and it comforted her little. She couldn't mail the letter without asking Dirk's uncle for his address. She didn't want to do that.

She liked Dirk's uncle and there was no reason why she shouldn't ask for the address. No reason except that she felt shy at the thought of speaking to anyone about Dirk.

CHAPTER 34 ❦

Each morning by the road was like nearly every other morning. One morning the girl saw a bluebird with his mate. It must be growing cold up north. It really was hard to realize that all sorts of different things were happening in the world beyond the mountains. Where Dirk was now there might be snow, or rain falling on fields that she would never see.

Thousands of miles beyond mountains and oceans people were frightened of war. The girl's mother and father talked excitedly about the news they heard over the radio. All the war talk made the girl think that she hated humanity. Of all animals, she thought, man is the cruelest and the most destructive.

The queer thing was that when she thought of certain individuals she felt as loving as God. People in general seemed hateful, but she felt altogether different about the ones she knew. Especially those who were having a hard time. Sometimes she heard stories about people that made her feel warm with pity and love. Like about the poor woman who lived up the road.

She was a spiritless-looking woman and she had four children. There was a boy of ten, a girl of six, and twins just learning to walk. The father was seldom home. Where he spent his time or wages no one seemed to know. From the thin look of the children it was evident that little money was spent on them.

But the twins owned a treasure. The twins had a goat and without the milk from that goat the twins might not have lived. The goat's name was Skipper. She had been given to the family when the twins were very little.

The mother and the children were devoted to Skipper. Skipper seemed devoted to them. She followed the children when they played outdoors and she ate whatever she could find to eat. Last spring when rains were hard Skipper was brought into the kitchen. No one could have been happy by the warm stove if the goat had been left to shiver in the rain.

But for all the goat's friendliness she would not let the mother milk her. The boy couldn't milk her either. The father was home at such uncertain times that the goat would go dry if she were left for him to milk.

A friendly neighbor got into the habit of going every night to milk the goat.

Because the woman was alone so much she was glad to see the neighbor come. The milking of the goat became a rite. Every night when the man came the whole family turned out to watch the milking. If the children were asleep the mother woke them and bundled them in their ragged bedclothes. The boy carried one baby and the mother carried the other. The little girl walked ahead proudly carrying the lantern.

They didn't talk much. It seemed satisfying just to stand quietly and watch the man milk the goat.

The neighbor usually laughed when he told the story. But somehow it made the girl sad. It made her feel friendly toward that woman whom she hardly knew.

CHAPTER 35 ⌒

"Sunday quiet" was an expression that had no meaning these days. The two words were beautiful together; they made the girl think of sunshine, a silent countryside, and a sweet bell ringing in a white church steeple.

Once those words had meant just that. Even the barnyard noises had seemed quieter. The crowing of roosters and cackling of hens were drowsy sounds. Save for the harnessing up for the drive to church, the barns were quiet; horses could loaf all afternoon in the pasture. The girl liked to think of mothers and fathers and neat children starting off to church. After that, Sunday dinner, probably company, and a long lazy afternoon until chore time.

But now Sunday was the noisiest day of the week. It wasn't a day of rest, it was a day of travel. Sunday was the girl's special day for realizing that she didn't like people.

Her quiet road was a thoroughfare on Sundays. It was out of curiosity that folks drove along it. They drove too fast to see any of its beauty. In the early morning men and boys drove along shooting rabbits from their cars. They were able to see the rabbits but not to see "No Hunting" signs.

The girl had to watch her cattle closely: any animal that crossed the road was in danger. People drove fast and tooted horns without slowing down when they saw things in the way.

She felt a special contempt for city dwellers who brought picnic lunches and left beer cans and paper plates where only clean earth and dry grass should be. They threatened the countryside by building fires. They made a great deal of noise. If they climbed a steep hill they could not bear to see the vastness of mountains and valleys making them seem so insignificant. They shouted and whistled and sang. The girl was sure that some people never climbed a hill without being noisy at the summit. They were disturbed by great beautiful quietness; they had to make known the fact that they were the lords of creation.

One Sunday morning the cows she drove slowed and stopped curiously. Flaxie pushed ahead to see what was there, and whinnied and looked back to see what Pete thought. Pete looked scornful.

The girl saw two Indian ponies standing with trailing reins. Beside the road were their masters, sleeping deeply. The smell of whisky was strong. She looked with pity at the sleepers. The early morning was bitterly cold, night had been colder. Yet they had been too drunk to hunt shelter, or even to cover themselves with saddle blankets. They would suffer when they woke stiff and aching. The girl stopped long enough to unbridle the ponies and hang the bridles over the saddle horns. The patient animals were hungry. Now they could graze, or wander home if they chose. When the Indians wakened they wouldn't remember whether they had unbridled their ponies or let them stand. If the ponies went on the Indians would have to walk home and maybe that would limber them up.

The girl stared at the relaxed faces. There was certainly something childlike about the men huddled on the cold earth. Sleep gave their faces an innocent look. Their clothes were torn and dirty. She smiled down at them compassionately and followed her cows along the road.

When she drove the cows home the Indians and their ponies were gone. Ahead of her, the cows' split hoofs obliterated tracks, so she couldn't tell whether the men had ridden home or had had to walk. If they had walked their footprints would probably have appeared uncertain, wavering back and forth across the road.

If the drunken sleepers that Sunday morning had been white men she would have felt disgust. But the Indians had seemed like children trying to have a good time. It was too bad their fun should end so miserably.

CHAPTER 36 ⌒

One morning a stray bull came swaggering up the road to meet the girl's cows. He grumbled and roared and shook his heavy head. There was no time to chase Joseph toward home. Joseph saw the stranger and wanted to fight him.

Both bulls stood still, turned their heads sideways, and blew through their noses. The cows watched with interest. So did the girl. She didn't want the bulls to fight, but there was no easy way to stop them, so she would umpire the battle. The bulls were of the same size, their horn spread was equal. If one had been a muley she would have felt duty bound to prevent a clash; the horned one would have too much advantage. As it was, she didn't think either one could do much damage to the other. She hoped Joseph would be the victor.

For only a little while the bulls stood blowing and looking sideways at each other. They charged at the same time. There was a clash of horns. Forehead to forehead they pushed. It was a fine sight, those heavy animals, their legs braced, their heads lowered.

Then, step by step, Joseph gave ground. Excitedly the girl shouted advice and encouragement. She felt she couldn't stand it to see Joseph vanquished. The other pushed harder and faster. Joseph was walking backward at incredible speed. He seemed to dance backward. He gave a quick turn of his head, he charged forward, and the stranger received a blow in the side that made him bellow. Joseph followed up with a good hard shove that sent his opponent through the barbed-wire fence by the roadside. Wires snapped, a fence post leaned, and Joseph was in the field with his enemy. The strange bull recovered his feet and fought with valor. Again they clashed horns and pushed, they got on their knees and wrangled, too breathless for battle cry or muttered challenge. At last they gave up for an interval to rest.

"We'll call it a draw," the girl told them, and stepped Pete over the fence wires. She chased Joseph back to the road, and sent the stranger off across the field. Both bulls began to swear. The girl took Joseph home. "I don't think we'll call it a draw after all," she told him. "You're the one that made him bawl; besides, you shoved him off your road."

That didn't comfort Joseph. In his corral he grumbled half the day away.

The girl thought fondly that it was wonderful how a calf as tiny and bewildered as Joseph had been could grow into such a power. She wished that his mother could know.

Joseph's mother was an old cow when he was born. People will tell you that old cows' calves are stiff eared. But

Joseph's father was a young bull, and the offspring of an old and a young parent is apt to be both sturdy and wise.

Blossom had had so many calves the girl couldn't remember them all. Her heifers had been raised, her bull calves fattened for veal. The old cow was a loving mother, and she had grieved bitterly each time one of her sons was sold. Before Joseph was born she had had two bulls in a row. Now she seemed worried, as if she remembered the loss of her last two calves. It seemed that she loved this new little bull more than any calf she had borne. She would not hide him and go peacefully off to graze. She was never more than two steps from him. From the day he was born to the day she died he was never out of her sight.

When the calf was about two weeks old his mother grew sick. The girl and her father dosed the cow with all the remedies they knew. She kept growing worse. The horse doctor came and said there was little he could do. The cow had obeyed a natural instinct and eaten the after-birth. People who ought to know better will tell you that a cow eats afterbirth for medicinal purposes. The truth is that a cow, like an untamed animal, eats offal from birth in order to try and keep her young a secret. She is afraid some wild animal might find the afterbirth and then start looking for a newborn creature. Many cows dispose of the afterbirth with no ill effects. But Blossom was so old her digestive organs had weakened.

Old Blossom stretched out dull eyed, her calf resting near. Late in the afternoon the little bull grew hungry. He stood up and bawled loudly. He walked to his mother and moved around her, poking and prodding her with his nose, putting his forehead against her side and pushing. He did his best to make her get up and feed him. As he grew hungrier he grew more worried. He bawled louder and more frantically. He braced his little hoofs and pushed the old cow with all his might.

The girl lifted the cow's head from the earth and held it in her arms. The calf lipped at his mother's ears. The cow tried to lick him. It was all she could do; she could never rise again.

"We'll raise your little calf for you," the girl promised.

Joseph soon forgot his loss when he was taken to another cow to be fed. In two months he was so fat he seemed to bounce when he ran.

The girl's father looked at the rollicksome young bull and said, "Prime veal."

The girl said, "Remember how he tried to get old Blossom up."

They couldn't forget the sad little calf moving around his sick mother. Now here he was, a great roaring bull, who would probably be with them until he died of old age. But, anyway, he was a good bull, and sired lusty calves. If he became a bad bull they'd have to put up with him somehow. A promise to the dying is something sacred, even if the dying is only a cow.

CHAPTER 37

A neighbor drove past the girl and her cows one morning. She smiled and nodded at him, and he nodded without smiling and looked a little annoyed because he had to slow down for a heifer on the road.

This man never looked happy.

He believed, without a shade of doubt, that when good Christian people died they went to a better world. The good were rewarded beyond their greatest expectations, and the bad were justly punished. The Lord would take care of His own, and when this man's crops failed or his calves sickened he knew that the Lord was only trying him. His faith was strong as a mountain, no matter what happened. He ruled his children sternly, and his young daughters hated him. He strove earnestly to save their souls. He also tried to save his neighbors'.

In church he was so full of the Spirit of the Lord that he shouted Amen at regular intervals. At prayer meeting he testified with ardor; his prayers were long reminders to the Almighty. God mustn't be allowed to forget that He had promised to reward the good and punish the wicked.

This man said that every hour he was grateful because Jesus had shed His blood for him.

He was a mystery to the girl.

Just imagine, she thought, knowing that there is no such thing as death. Knowing for sure that sometime you would be reunited with people you loved who had died. Knowing that God was watching you with kind and loving eyes, ready to catch you should you stumble. Imagine a shining world all ready to receive you when you died. People, time out of mind, had pondered the secret of living and dying—what comfort to know for sure the riddle of creation!

Imagine knowing all these glorious facts and going about with an unhappy face!

The man's miserable expression had almost put a blight on the golden morning. She had been feeling glad because she was alive and could see sunshine on brown leaves. Now with unseeing eyes she watched two ground squirrels chasing round and round. She watched them dully before she actually saw them. Then she laughed. What a world, when the passing of a man who believes himself a Christian made you feel gloomy for a while.

When she was little the girl had been sent to Sunday school. By the time she was fifteen years old she wouldn't go any longer. She didn't like being taught that people had souls, and animals didn't. She could never believe that animals were created for no other reason than the use of mankind. "If that's so," she argued, "why were animals on the earth for thousands of years before there were humans?" And she added, "I'll bet a flea thinks that a dog is made for it to bite."

She questioned the minister. "If Christ was so compassionate, why didn't he say more about suffering animals?"

It seemed to her then that when Jesus said, "Come unto Me all ye who are weary and heavy laden and I will give you rest," he should have been speaking about tired workhorses.

It was well for Jesus to say, "In my Father's house are many mansions," but he also should have spoken of a heaven of many meadows for tired and hungry horses, for driven sheep and cattle. He should have promised a refuge for the fox run to earth and torn apart by hounds.

The minister thought she was being irreverent. People *were* weary and overburdened, he said reasonably.

Yes, said the girl, but they could speak up for themselves. And when they spoke up for themselves they did such bad things that you felt they deserved to be overworked and starved. "Look at the French Revolution," she said dramatically. "'Look how the Russians treated the poor women and children of the royal family."

"I know how you feel," the minister said kindly, "but don't worry your head about too many things."

But at that age she would worry her head about too many things. She announced that she was through with religion forever. Her mother said, "Religion is something that each individual must settle for himself."

So the girl settled it, and became a lost soul. Being lost didn't trouble her at all. She was glad not to have to go to Sunday school any longer.

The world outdoors was full of marvelous and curious things. People could take religion for granted, along with Sunday clothes, but the girl could never take nature for granted.

When a cat pounced at a lizard and the lizard cast off its wiggling tail in one direction and ran to safety in another, the girl found herself thinking, "How smart God is." She watched the cat chase after the lively tail instead of the living lizard. For a long time the tail kept acting as though it had a mind of its own. The girl took the twisting thing in her hand to look at its clever design. The end that had been fastened to the lizard had five little white spikes, like teeth. They had evidently been dovetailed into similar spikes, and the lizard had only to give a certain twist or shake to turn it loose. Now the lizard had better be cautious until a new tail was grown.

All her life the girl was going to be a very reverent person.

CHAPTER 38 ❧

By Fernstone Canyon there were a few acres of level land where brown grass stood tall. The barbed-wire fence sagged so that the cows easily stepped over it and soon they were grazing as though they had been starving for just this particular plot of dry grass. Joseph saw a clump of green juicy milkweed and he made certain joyous sounds. The cows hurried around him like hens gathering around a rooster that has found something good.

The girl was uncertain whether to drive them out or not. This wasn't roadside grass, this was grass on private land. There was a time when she wouldn't have dared let her cows even as much as look over the fence.

But now, who was to drive her out? She gloated just a little. The only thing that would try to drive her out might be the ghost of old Jenks. She walked to the fire-blackened remains of Jenks's house and sat down under some pepper trees that had once been scorched almost to death. It gave her pleasure to see how the trees had managed to come back to life after they had been so badly seared. A pepper tree won't give up easily.

She sat in the dark shade and thought of how mad old Jenks would be if he could see her cows now. She almost wished his ghost was hovering around. She was quite sure that some of the Indians thought his ghost still lingered; some of them believed that he had set fire to his house after he had died.

"I don't feel as sorry for him as I should," she thought. "It's good to see old Whitey eating this grass."

Before Whitey was such an old cow she once got a spell of being breachy. Fences couldn't hold her, and for some perverse reason, every time she broke out she made for Jenks's place.

Old Jenks would not tolerate any stray animal. What was his was his, and he wouldn't give a mouthful of even dry foxtails to any beast he did not own. The girl used to wish that Jenks's stock would get out just once. He kept his work horse hobbled all the time it was in pasture, and his cow had to wear a poke. One morning he found Whitey in his corn patch and shot at her. He told the girl that next time his aim would be better. The girl didn't doubt that; it was known that Jenks had shot two stray Indian ponies.

He would say, every time he saw the girl, that she ought to get rid of that old white cow. The girl told him it was none of his business whether she kept Whitey or not. She sounded brave, but she was frightened for she knew that Jenks would harm the cow if he got angry enough. He wouldn't hesitate to put out poison for her as he did for dogs and cats and squirrels.

Mrs. Jenks was as hard looking as her husband. He was a big fat red-faced man, she was a short fat wrinkle-faced woman. She and her husband dressed alike in blue denim overalls. They never went anywhere except to town for mail and supplies, so Mrs. Jenks had no need for pretty clothes. She had no need for them, but the girl learned that she wanted them. Mrs. Jenks looked unfriendly, but the girl found her to be a very friendly person.

If the girl rode by when old Jenks wasn't around Mrs. Jenks would come out to talk to her. She was hungry for talk, woman talk. She would have liked to belong to the Ladies' Aid where she could sit and sew and talk about things women understood.

"Why don't you join?" asked the girl.

"Jenks won't have it."

"Well, you aren't a prisoner, are you?"

"Just about. Jenks won't let me have no money. Not even my own butter-and-egg money. He's got lots of money, too. Sold out two dairies when the doctor made him quit work. But he won't give me a cent. Without a cent of her own a woman is same as in jail."

"I'd demand my rights," said the girl.

"You can't cross him. The doctor said it would be the same as murder." Mrs. Jenks touched her bosom significantly. "His heart. Get him too worked up and he has an attack."

"Well, Whitey and I have made him mad and he didn't die of it."

"Tisn't good for him, though."

The girl wanted to say that Jenks might as well be dead. Mrs. Jenks seemed to read her thoughts. "He was good to me once, though it was long ago. Seems like I have to pay him back for that all the rest of my days."

"But no reason why you shouldn't associate with folks and have a good time. Why does he make you stay at home so much?"

"It's his way. Guess he don't know any better. He says he's ashamed of me. I had a hard time of it after my first husband died. Jenks came along, and, well…I was just about picked up off the streets. He reminds me of it when he gets mad."

"That was a long time ago," comforted the girl. "I'll bet you always did the best you could. Was your first husband nice?"

"No, he drank himself to death. I was married to that one when I was only fifteen."

The girl sighed. It seemed as though Mrs. Jenks never had had any fun and never would. As far as she knew she was the only friend Mrs. Jenks had, the only woman who ever talked to her.

That was why Mrs. Jenks hurried up the road to the girl's house the night Jenks died. The girl was wakened by hearing someone call her name. There was Mrs. Jenks at the door, an old coat pulled on over her nightgown. "Will you come help me?" she sobbed. "Jenks is awful sick! I don't know what to do."

The girl's father got out the car and drove Mrs. Jenks and the girl as far as Jenks's place and went on to town for the doctor. It was the first time the girl had been in the house. It was very dismal.

Jenks's eyes and mouth were open and he looked as though he were still in agony. He was dead, but his wife didn't know it. He lay on the bedroom floor, fully dressed, and Mrs. Jenks had put a pillow under his head. Now she held ammonia to his nose while she talked to the girl.

"I brought it on him," she said. "He stayed up late because he had got so he didn't sleep much. I had gone to sleep and then he came in and started to pick a quarrel. Said I stole a dime off him. I never. I shoulda not argued back, but I was so tired of his meanness. I felt as if I wanted his heart to hurt him. I just couldn't keep still. I done it a purpose. I got so mad I told him how I hated him and how I was going to steal all his money and run away. That was the first time I'd spoke up in years. He began shouting at me and then he keeled over. Seems like he ought to be coming out of it by now."

While Mrs. Jenks talked the girl kept listening for the sound of her father's car. The unhappy house and the dead man and Mrs. Jenks made her soul feel frozen.

She ran to the door when she heard the men. The doctor looked at Jenks and said there was nothing he could do. They lifted the body to the bed. Mrs. Jenks didn't seem to understand until the doctor spoke about going for the undertaker.

"Oh, no," she cried, "You've got to do something for him!" And she began unlacing Jenks's shoes and taking them off. She called him by his first name. "Ray," she kept repeating, "Oh, Ray."

Finally she spoke very sensibly. "Are you sure that he won't come to?"

The doctor said that nothing on earth could wake Jenks up again.

"Well, then," announced the widow, "I'm going to go through his pockets right now. But if he wakes up he'll kill me."

"He won't wake up," said the doctor gently.

"This'll wake him up if anything will," she said, and began to search the dead man.

What she found made even the doctor's eyes open wide. Old Jenks had been carrying nine thousand dollars around in the pockets of his overalls. Nine one-thousand dollar bills. The girl had never seen even a thousand dollars before.

"Now," said Mrs. Jenks, "I'm going to buy me a black silk dress to wear to the funeral. And a flowered silk one to wear for everyday."

The girl's father cleared his throat. "Why didn't he bank his money?"

"He didn't trust banks. He couldn't read and he couldn't write more than a cross for his name."

Then the girl felt full of pity. She felt sorry because she remembered riding past one day and seeing Jenks on the porch holding a paper. He had been pretending to read for the benefit of passers-by.

After the funeral Mrs. Jenks sold her cow and horse and chickens and moved to town. The house burned a few nights later. The Indians thought Jenks did it, but smarter folks said the widow did it to get the insurance.

November Grass

Now Jenks would surely turn in his grave if he could see the girl's cows enjoying themselves on his land. The cows eating his grass, and his wife spending his money. It would be hell for Jenks to see creatures enjoying the very things he had wanted to deny them.

CHAPTER 39 ⤚

The girl felt a little sleepy as she rested in the grass because she wasn't used to staying up later than nine o'clock. It must have been eleven before she ever got to bed last night. There was a movie in town about horses, all in color, and her father said it was a show they couldn't afford to miss. So the three of them went to see it after supper.

The picture was indeed beautiful. The girl never saw horses look so smooth and bright. The scenes of mares and colts were so tender the girl felt a hotness under her eyelids.

But what impressed her most was not the story on the screen, but the reaction of the audience to the story. It was a typical group of small-town dwellers and ranchers, like a cross section of California's rural people. As usual, a few reservation Indians were there. They liked to sit far front. More particular people sat far back, holding to the theory that there were too many fleas toward the front rows. That flea story worked on the girl's imagination so that she always felt itchy in any theater, even if she chanced to go to a movie in the city.

But that night she forgot all about the possibility of fleas. The picture was too beautiful and the audience too impressed. The story began at the time of the Civil War. It showed a horse farm in the South. Yankees came and took horses off to war, and the sad part was that it must have been spring, for all the mares had little colts. At the corral gates those heartless Yankees cut out the mares from the colts, and there the little colts were left to go hungry without their mammies' milk. You heard the mares calling frantically for their colts as they were driven down the road, and the poor colts ran crying wildly, trying to climb right through the bars of the corral. Gorgeous little thoroughbred colts, nickering for mothers gone off to war.

The girl became aware of a stifled sniffing and gulping all around. Furtively she watched the big man next to her. He brought out a handkerchief and blew his nose. He brushed his cheeks. There was something familiar about him, there in the dimness. Later she stole another look and saw who he was.

He lived across the valley. He was a careless loud-voiced man who could be heard afar when he swore at his cows. She had never known that he had any feeling for animals. He thought nothing of whacking a calf on the head and cutting its throat in front of its trembling mother.

She felt herself smile at him tenderly in the darkness; she loved him because his heart was breaking over the orphan colts.

Going to that movie had done her more good than going to church. It had made her feel compassionate toward people.

She thought of the butcher who came one day to buy calves. She didn't think he could have any sympathy at all. Every fall he took time off from killing cattle to kill deer. She could understand that the killing of calves was merely a business proposition with him, but it vexed her to think that when he took a vacation he did more killing. He was as bad as the veterinary who spent eleven months of the year trying to save animals' lives, and one month trying to see how much game he could bag.

The time the butcher came there was a litter of kittens in the barn. They had just reached that enchanting soft age when their violet eyes were wide open, and they made playful lunges at every shadow that stirred. When the butcher saw them they were rolling in the sunshine, batting at each other's tails with tiny folded paws.

The big man sat down on the barn floor and picked up a kitten. It was smaller than his hand. He held it against his check and laughed when it patted at his eyelashes.

"If you ain't the cutest thing," he told it. He reached for another and perched it on his shoulder and felt its whiskers tickle his ear. "Never seen such pretty kitten-cats."

He wiggled his finger along the floor and a striped kitten pounced on it: "Prettier than any young thing, ain't they? Prettier than little lions or tigers. Look at that paw, now." He held a paw between his fingers and studied it. "So tiny and soft. Ain't they little and helpless?"

The girl was entranced. She said, "Pick out the prettiest, I'll save it for you."

The butcher sighed wistfully, like a child. "I'd love to have one. But my wife, she just can't abide cats."

CHAPTER 40 ⌒

One morning before the girl started out her mother sighed and said, "Poor child." Every morning her mother looked at her as if she were thinking "poor child," but she didn't always say it.

Her mother thought it was a pity that a young girl gave all her time to cattle and horses. "But I like it this way," the girl had told her over and over again.

"Look at your hands," her mother said.

Mother couldn't understand. The girl felt as if she should protect her mother from the harder things. And her mother was always trying to protect her.

The girl felt a sense of accomplishment when she did a difficult job. If she came home tired from some adventure of driving cattle or rounding up stray horses her mother looked at her pityingly. She nearly cried when the girl came in late one stormy day in spring. The girl was dripping rain and so cold she couldn't keep her teeth still. She was tired and her back ached. Her wet clothes were covered with mud. But in spite of all her discomfort she was inwardly glowing with happiness. She had worked hard in the storm and she had done what she had set out to do. She told her mother all that had happened, so her mother could see just how it was and why she felt triumphant. Her mother tried to understand, but all the time she was thinking how much she herself would have hated being out in the wet and cold and coming darkness.

"But I loved it, really I did," the girl told her.

Her mother thought she was just saying that to be brave, and kissed her and said she was a gallant child.

It had been raining hard all day and when the girl went out late in the afternoon she saw that one of the springing heifers was missing. That meant that the heifer had hidden herself to calve. If the girl had realized that Jenny was due so soon she would have kept her in the barn. She hadn't expected the calf for at least a week, and now Jenny had gone off in the storm and was either in labor, or already was hidden somewhere with a shivering calf. Hundreds of California calves and colts are born in the rain every spring. But the girl wouldn't feel comfortable unless Jenny and her calf were safe in the barn, because the rain was fierce and snow was on the mountains.

The springing heifers were kept in a small pasture near the river where they had trees and brush for shelter. In this pasture it should not be hard to find a heifer who had calved before her time. The girl walked around the pasture, searching every leafy place, stopping to listen for the sound of Jenny moaning if in labor, or lowing to the calf. But against the hard rain, and the wind in the leaves, and the roaring of the streams, Jenny would have to speak up loudly to be heard.

The girl had her head tied in a heavy scarf. She wore a raincoat and her overalls were tucked into rubber boots, so she felt comfortable and happy to be out looking for the heifer.

But after she had covered most of the little pasture she grew anxious. Some heifers, when their time is upon them, start wandering and go as far as they can before the calf is born. The girl followed the fence and came to a place where the wire was loosened, and there were a few brown hairs from Jenny's coat. Beyond was a hoof mark, already filled with water.

Somewhere in the tangle of brush and wild-rose vines by the riverbed Jenny was hiding. She might not have picked a safe spot; her calf might be resting too near the rising water.

The girl tried to follow the hoof marks but the rain had dimmed them. Besides, this river bottom land was pasture for a neighbor's heifers, and there could be a multitude of tracks not Jenny's. She tried to think what she would do if she were the heifer and she was quite sure she would head for a thicket. She hoped Jenny hadn't tried to cross the river.

For an hour she plodded through the brush, and the rain grew heavier. Her raincoat was no protection now, the scarf about her head had soaked up all the rain it could hold, water was running into her ears and down her neck. She pulled off the scarf and felt better.

There were deep depressions in the sand by the river.
Some cow had crossed, and it might be Jenny. And it might
not. She couldn't tell for sure—she might have missed the
heifer in the brush.

The river was not wide and not very deep, but it was
swift and dark. She couldn't see the bottom. She stood
looking across it. The white rain was like a veil. Then she
wasn't sure, she thought a bush moved on the other side.

Because of the storm, darkness was coming early. She
began to wade in the water. Before she had gone far it was
over her boot tops. She tried to feel ahead with each step;
she was afraid of walking into a hole. After a while the
water was waist high, and then when she was halfway over
it grew shallower.

The bush wasn't a bush. It was Jenny. Her calf was
trembling on the wet sand. The girl sank down beside it.
Jenny nosed them both. She licked the calf and she licked
the girl, making low anxious sounds.

"You'd better be worried," the girl told her.

It was a pity Jenny hadn't had sense enough to stay
in the shelter of low trees or brush. The calf might have
been dropped in the river. The girl couldn't imagine why
Jenny had wanted to wade the river.

The calf was a little heifer and very weak. When the
girl stood it up, it toppled over. Warm milk in its stomach
was what it needed. She propped it up again and pushed it
to Jenny's udder. Jenny kept backing to look at it. She was
in a state of confusion. She was pleased with her calf, but
she was too excited to know that she must stand still and
let it nurse.

It couldn't be left in the rain all night, hungry and cold. If it couldn't gather strength to stand and nurse, the storm would be too much for it.

It was almost the color of the sand, and its eyes stared dimly without seeing anything. It had long lashes. Its ears were like flower petals. They twitched in the rain.

The girl gave the newborn calf her finger. Sucking on something seemed to comfort it. Its soft tongue gripped and pulled.

Suddenly it was as though the storm decided to demolish this frail new calf. Such a flood of wind-driven rain came that the girl bent her body over the little animal, and the mother grew frightened and bawled. The roaring of the river, the sound of rain, the wind in the trees made the mother's voice sound like the feeble cry of a calf. The girl huddled over the newborn and endured the storm's beating, thinking it would be less fierce in a minute.

Even if the rain hadn't been blinding, it had grown almost too dark to see. The storm and the coming night were allied, as if determined to keep the calf from living.

She gathered up the calf. It was not heavy. But she knew about carrying calves. A calf seems light when you first pick it up; then it grows heavier with every step. She showed the calf to its mother, so Jenny would know to follow.

"Come, Jenny," she said, and started wading. Jenny kept crowding against her. The girl gripped the calf tighter, hugging it against her as if that would still its shivering. No rain or river or wind should wrench it from her.

With her boots full of water, each step in the river was hard work. Though she hugged the calf tightly as she could, it kept slipping a little lower. She thought of the waist-deep place to be got through somehow. She tried shifting the calf higher again, and nearly dropped it.

She kept thinking, "Just one step more." The width of the river at once was too much to think about. But a step at a time was not impossible. She was careful to keep the calf's head up. It was already so wet that the rest of it didn't matter.

She didn't fall until she had passed the deepest place. Head and all they both went under for an instant. The mother grew alarmed and pushed and the girl almost went down again. She was as shaky as the calf when she floundered to shore.

After a while she felt stronger. She felt exultant the last mile when she had the light from her mother's window to guide her. It was a long mile, and she had to stop often to put down the calf and rest.

When the cow was content in the barn, and the calf rubbed dry and fed, the girl felt comfort like a wool blanket around her. Though she stood dripping and shivering and weary in her mother's kitchen she was happy in her heart.

"Poor child," her mother said.

And the girl said, "Poor mother."

CHAPTER 41 ᔪ

For all her gentleness mother had strength. It must take strength to fit into a way of living that you did not like. And find beauty, too, in that way of living.

Because she thought the girl worked too hard, the mother felt a tiredness. All the time the girl was out in the rain after the calf, her mother was fighting the storm. Walking up and down, looking out the windows, wishing her husband would come in from milking so she could send him out to find the girl. She imagined dangers that didn't exist. The girl was doing a difficult thing, but not a dangerous thing. To the mother the storm seemed wicked and destructive. The girl had felt the rain a personal thing bent on destroying a weak calf. The mother felt the same way, only she worried about the girl, not the calf.

But for all her anxiety mother was even tempered most of the time. Seldom had the girl seen her angry about anything. If the girl disapproved of certain conditions as strongly as she felt her mother did, she knew that she would have raged sometimes.

Now, the girl mused, life is a sort of cycle. She thought about Dirk. If Dirk had wanted her she would probably have gone with him. Most of the time she would have lived in a city and tried to live Dirk's kind of life. Like her mother she would be living where she did not want to live. She wondered if she would have continued to love Dirk then; she wondered if she would have been as faithful to him and his ways as her mother had been to her father.

It would be a strange turning of fate—a mother living a country life and not liking it, a daughter living a city life and not liking it. Each longing for what the other had.

California is full of homesick people. Old folks longing for homes "back east in Texas." Or Illinois or Wisconsin. Some even from New England, where hills are stony, too, but wearing more leaves than these stony hills.

Now when her mother thought of home back east she thought of a gentle place with dogwood blossoms white in May, and pussy willows gray and soft as their name. Maybe she forgot about winter blizzards. It is said that when the homesick ones go east they are still homesick. Nothing is so lovely as the way it is remembered.

And I, thought the girl, if I were back there I'd be hungry for the smell of sagebrush, and longing for brown hills, and wishing to see cows eating gray November grass like this. How much would I love Dirk then?

She thought how it would be if Dirk were dead. No different from now. It seemed as if she were never going to see Dirk or hear from him again. For her he was dead.

Yet she could shut her eyes and see him just as he looked. She could feel that bewilderment that came when she had most wanted him.

She wondered how much her mother knew about the way she felt. They had each been careful about speaking of Dirk. "Seems to be a nice boy," her mother said. "He is a gentleman. Not like the kind of boys around here."

And the girl answered, "Oh, he's a lot of fun."

Sometimes her mother had a way of looking at her that made the girl feel that mother knew more than she said out loud. There was comfort in that. Though there were times when she had longed to creep to her mother in the night and talk about love, and cry, she was glad she never had. About such matters you ought to have pride. It was more comforting to have her mother know, without spoken words.

But if Dirk should come back and want her, that would be different. Then she wouldn't know what to do.

She knew that she would want Dirk. And she knew that she would want to keep all that she had now. But she couldn't have everything.

Only her mother knew whether it would be worthwhile to give up one way of living and try a strange way. Someday she would know for sure about her mother, and it would be because of Dirk that she would know.

CHAPTER 42 ⋍

Far off some bull sent a challenging call into the clear morning air. It made Joseph shake his head and rumble and toss dirt over his shoulder with one splayed front hoof. In the dust by the road's edge he uncovered something which might have been there for centuries.

The girl picked up an arrowhead. It was beautiful as a jewel, for in this land Indians made many arrowheads of quartz. This one sparkled like frost. Its matrix was a design of three slanting red parallel lines. The girl turned it over and over, feeling its sharpness as once an Indian hand had felt it with satisfaction. He had made it with painstaking care, that unknown Indian, and he must have delighted in its beauty as well as in its trueness. Now both he and his quarry had disappeared and only this fragile thing endured to prove that once a certain Indian lived.

An Indian who had quenched his thirst at a spring where the girl had drunk many times, who hunted the ancestors of deer she might have seen, whose eyes were familiar with the shapes of all these hills...She held the chipped quartz and felt the age of hills and the briefness of human life. The animals had been the true owners of the hills for eons; then Indians had owned the land and hunted the animals. In time strange white people declared themselves owners. After their hour was done, the animals might multiply again, and sagebrush cover the fields. Or maybe some other, stronger form of life might rule.

Except for insignificant scars, the low hills and the high mountains would be unchanged. Except for a few buildings, fences and fields in the valley, the land was as the Indian had seen it. Had he seen it as a beautiful place, or as only part of a familiar scene? The girl couldn't count the times in her life when she had climbed the pasture hill and looked at valley and mountains. In early morning, at noon, at sundown, in summer and winter and spring and fall— and never had it been commonplace. When the sun was low a certain gold light came into the valley; there would be sharp lines where shadow and sunshine met on slopes of hills, and bare rocky mountains glowed with color.

This was her own land. She thought it was home. This had been home to deer and coyote, snake and bird. It had been home to him who fashioned the shining arrowhead. Here he had slept, hunted and eaten. He had quarreled, made love, begotten children. Charred remains of his bones might be buried in a shallow place in the hills. His descendants might be among those who lived up the valley on the reservation.

Almost anywhere, if you looked, you could find things Indians had left. Hollows were pounded in stones where women had ground acorns into meal. Small stones had been placed on boulders as markers that meant certain things. Some signs meant "water near." Some were to show where food had been stored.

Whenever the girl found any of these things she felt a strange excitement. Because of its shortness life seemed exceedingly valuable. She wanted to be aware of every blessed moment of it. Everything seemed important when she thought she had so little time to live. Some people might feel inclined to shrug their shoulders and say, "What does it matter? We'll all be dead a hundred years from now." But the girl thought that that was what made it matter.

She was forever sorry for young animals whose lives were taken, yet she could live only a little time longer than they. Such a very little taste of life you had, and whether you were hungry for more, or found it bitter, didn't matter. It was snatched away and, as far as you knew, there was no other chance to savor it.

She hoped that the Indian who had so cleverly fashioned this triangle of stone had had a good time of it. He had made himself be thought of by his skill. The girl believed that he had done more than she would do. When she died, there would be nothing of her own making to show that she had lived. With her hands she would make no enduring or useful thing.

CHAPTER 43 ⌐

The horses the girl had seen in the movie were beautiful, but none was lovelier than Flaxie. The sunshine intensified the burning sorrel of her coat, the pale gold of her mane and tail. Every move the filly made was quick. If she wanted the girl to give her a lump of sugar she rushed up trembling with eagerness. If she only shook her forelock out of her eyes it was an intense gesture. When she stamped at flies she did it with all her heart.

It was exactly a year ago that the girl had first seen Flaxie. Flaxie was only a few hours old. She was nursing her mother intently, her frizzled tail switching back and forth. Watching her, the girl thought that in all the world there is no line as beautiful as the turned curve of the neck of a nursing foal.

The girl knew the colt's mother and her owner. The man had sent word that morning that the colt was born, and the girl had hurried to see it. She didn't know then that she was ever going to own Flaxie.

All that day the girl watched the foal and its mother. Young foals are different from any other young animals. There is more mystery and magic about them. Even the sturdy little workhorse colts have a fragile, indescribably delicate look. New colts still seem to belong to the spirit world. Their mothers seem to sense this. A mother mare acts as though she feels that her colt might sprout wings and fly away like Pegasus. Mother mares seem to hear wing beats all about. Flaxie's mother was having beautiful dreams. Lights burned in her eyes; she would stand entranced for minutes, looking afar and nickering velvet sounds.

Flaxie's mother was an ordinary bay mare. She was as handsome as the average mare with no especially fine points. But she was beautiful the day her foal was born.

The bay mare had been running in the hills back of the Indian reservation when the colt was conceived. The stallion was a sorrel, with a blazed face and two white socks. He was almost a legendary animal; no one had ever caught him, or even ridden close to him. Near every rural community there seems to be one such animal. The girl had heard men say, of some colt, that the mother was just an ordinary cow horse, but the father was the wild stallion that ran back in the hills. "Must have had racehorse blood, because there wasn't anyone could run him down. We like to run our horses to death chasing him."

Men loved talking of a wild stallion. Though they spoke as though they would like to see the horse properly corraled and tamed, they took pride in speaking of his freedom. Horses as wild as deer were exciting to even the most unimaginative ranch hand.

The girl wondered if it was because man himself has lost his freedom that he likes to think of untamed stallions.

At any rate, the colt seemed more precious to her because of wild blood in its veins. The mare soon grew used to having the girl near and didn't try to herd the colt away. After the colt nursed, it stretched out on the ground and the girl crept up to it and rested beside it. It breathed quick little breaths. Once its nostrils quivered and it nickered in its sleep, as if it were dreaming. The girl wondered what dreams a new colt could have.

Its body was short and round, its legs thin. When it stood up it was hunched, as though someone had given it a good hard spank on its rump. There was something dolphinlike about the line of neck and head. Seeing a new colt always made the girl think of sea horses. The forehead had an earnest bulge. Later it would smooth out, the body become better proportioned. The little animal was beautiful now but it held promise of more beauty.

Flaxie slept most of that day with her head on the girl's lap. When she grew hungry she opened her eyes slowly, stretched, considered her unruly legs, and finally planned how to get up and nurse. Seeing the eyes come open interested the girl. The pale blue eye and the dark brown eye seemed unrelated and unfocused. Awareness came into the eyes as wakefulness came into the rest of the body. A wavering nicker announced hunger, and the mother answered to say that she was right here, her udder swollen.

Before that day was over the colt had had a try at running and playing in a half-clumsy, half-graceful way. The mother watched with anxious pride, whickering cautions;

the girl was equally proud and delighted. "Darling little foal," she kept saying, and the mare seemed to say the same thing.

Now the girl remembered that day tenderly and was glad the mare had had happiness for a time. It seemed almost like fate that the girl and the mare had shared the colt's first day. It made the colt belong to both of them.

The mare was old and when a cold rain came she took pneumonia and died. When the girl heard that she started worrying about the colt. Who would trouble to get up in the night to feed it from a bottle? Young colts need milk so often that hardly anyone succeeds in raising a sturdy one by hand. Most bottle-fed colts grow into rickety-looking pot-bellied yearlings.

The girl had no peace until she persuaded her father to trade a heifer for the colt. She was very glad that Flaxie was a fall colt, because by weaning time the green grass would be nourishing.

Flaxie had called for her mother until she was hoarse. When she tried to whinny she made little squawking bird-like sounds. She was very nearly named Bird instead of Flaxie. But any colt could be named Bird. Flaxie belonged to one with white gold mane and tail.

At first a rubber nipple was distasteful to the colt. But when she grew hungry enough she was glad to suck on it, and soon the sight of the girl coming with a bottle of milk had the same meaning for her as had the sight of her mother. In a few days she was believing that the girl was her mother, and she talked to the girl as a colt talks to the mother mare. The girl whistled a certain low whistle for

Flaxie, and when Flaxie heard it she began hurrying, and nickering every step of the way until her lips took the rubber nipple. She always drank like one starved, her blue eye and her brown eye blissfully half-closed. When every drop was gone she stood bewildered for a minute, and then whinnied for more. Feeding her often and not too much at a time was the best way. So on those cold nights the girl left her bed to go to the barn. When she whistled she heard Flaxie scrambling up, and Flaxie's white face came toward her in the dimness. There was no coldness in the night then, only warm feelings of love.

Before weaning time Flaxie had had gallons of warm sugared milk and pounds of rolled barley. But not a drop of milk or a grain of barley had been wasted, because the colt had developed as beautifully as though she had been with her own mother all the time.

Being a colt's foster mother was an experience the girl wouldn't have missed. It had taught her the feeling of a mare for a colt, of a colt for its mother. She had learned the way of a colt's growing mind so that she had a knowledge of horses she could not otherwise have had.

She couldn't even think of the colt without feeling all soft with love. No matter what could ever happen to Flaxie the girl couldn't lose her. Even if Flaxie should die, she would live, a golden bright picture in the girl's mind. It was comforting to think that there are some things that neither life nor death can take away.

CHAPTER 44 ⤳

The girl listened to the rustling sound of her cattle breaking the dry grass. They were aware of pleasure and pain,
good times and bad. The girl could share their feeling of
well-being, she could suffer when they suffered. Because
her life was bound up with the lives of animals depending
on her, she experienced more of living than if she had just
herself to consider.

She had done a lot of worrying over cows and horses,
but she had had a lot of pleasure, too. In the spring she felt
contented after the cows had calved, and she listened to the
soft mooing of mother cows. If she went to the barn on a
stormy night it was certainly a comforting thing to see animals looking soft and sleepy in the lantern light.

Now she was happy in a quiet sort of way, but she
didn't know how long it would last. Suppose the rains
didn't come, she thought, and all the dry grass was grazed
off? Or if old Whitey cow became desperately sick? And

now that men were hunting quail through the brush the hills might burn. There were always more fires in hunting season. The sound of shooting was enough to make her miserable, anyway. She couldn't help thinking of wounded quail creeping under leaves to die slowly. Now if she were to find a coyote in a trap in the riverbed she would feel as tortured as the animal.

So she felt she mustn't be smugly happy. Anything could happen to destroy her sense of peace.

The world was full of misery, yet everything wanted to be happy. Sometimes the girl felt that it might be one of the chief duties of the living to take pleasure in things the dead could no longer enjoy. To live dully might be a form of ingratitude to the long dead whose living and mating had made life possible for those who were now alive.

Each fall threatened to be a bad time. In spring when everything was exactly right, she felt that she couldn't bear to look ahead too far. Every time after a dry fall and a cold winter she felt so relieved that it was over that she didn't look forward with any pleasure to going through it all again. Then when she reached that time she took as much joy in colored leaves and purple mountains as she had taken in the young leaves in the spring. When she saw sycamore saplings beaded with leaf buds like drops of water she forgot how beautiful those same leaves would be when they were old and rust colored in November.

Now the cows ate the brittle November grass with as much relish as they had eaten the fresh grass of early summer. They were hungrier, so that every bite tasted good, dry and dusty as it was. She wondered if they remembered how sweet grass had tasted last spring. Did they remember when their calves were very little and the morning air was damp and warm?

It did not seem that summer was long ago. Cold nights replaced warm nights, there was a sharpness where there had been softness.

Remembering was part of the fun of living. Remembered spring made a November day more gracious. It was as if the future could be remembered before it happened: more springs would come and there would be other Novembers like this.

Now she was taking pleasure in warm sun and cool shadows, knowing that the cattle and Pete and Flaxie were finding enough to eat. They were happy.

The red cow's calf had showed the girl that happiness is instinctive with animals.

She had gone out one morning and found Rosie cleaning a limp calf. He hadn't tried to stand yet.

Sunshine, and the mother's constant licking, strengthened the little red bull so that after a while he began floundering around like a fish out of water. Each time he struggled his mother stood back and roared at him. His first instinct was to get to his feet, but after every try he had to take quite a long rest. Finally he got on his knees, his back legs propped up. There he swayed back and forth. With a little help he would succeed this time. The girl steadied him and he rose from his knees and stood on earth the first time. He didn't stand at all firmly, and it seemed he would surely go over when he tried to step.

His next instinct was to nurse his mother. His balance was threatened as soon as he began to move, but miraculously he managed to stay up while he poked his nose at the cow. By letting him suck her finger the girl guided him to a full teat, and like one famished, he began to suck. Being weak he constantly lost the teat, and the girl helped him find it again.

The more he drank the stronger he grew and when he had had enough he was not yet ready to drop down and sleep. The third instinct, that of play, was growing within him. While his mother lowed anxiously he galloped a few clumsy steps, then pranced with some grace, and tried a sharp turn, shaking his head. It was more than his legs would stand, and he went down. Again he floundered to rise, this time not for food, but for the fun of trying a few gamboling steps.

It made happiness seem important when you realized that the third thing this little red bull wanted to do was to play. It was as if he wanted to show his gladness because he was safely born, because he had risen and tasted milk, because the sunshine was dazzling after his nine months of darkness.

CHAPTER 45 ⌒

The girl thought that the intense clarity of the dry November air lent a clarity to her own thoughts. In the damp sweet air of spring she didn't see things as honestly as she did now. In spring she was befuddled with the soft prettiness of patterned fields. Now she looked at near brown hills and distant purple ones rising suppliant to the intense sunshine and her thoughts were as clearly defined as hills before the sky.

If she wakened in the night her thoughts were as sharp as the stars. Thoughts that worried her. Troublesome fears that prodded her mind so that she couldn't relax into drowsy contentment. Fears of drought prolonged everlastingly. What would happen if the time should come when there would be no grass anywhere?

Beyond that present fear came dark feelings about herself. What is to happen to me? She didn't know why such a thought should come in the night. Why should anything happen? But the years ahead of her looked many and uncertain. Things she had tried to forget came to her fierce-ly. She wakened to remember a young sheep that had been worried to death by dogs on a clear night. She tried never to think of that. But suddenly the feeling of it all came back to her, intense and horrible. All the terror of her little pet lamb wounded and struggling to escape. The body of the girl grew hot and cold; as if in a fever, she trembled and sweated. She had never felt such anguish, such despair.

It came to her that all lives end unhappily. No one who has led a happy life can die happily, for what happy person wants his days to end? How can the condemned be glad?

Were animals ever tortured by such heavy feelings of despair? In the middle of the night cows always got up and moved around a little and settled down again. Did old Whitey ever feel depressed when her joints ached these cold nights? The thought of a depressed cow made the girl smile, though it wasn't really funny. An old animal is piti-ful. Old horses with hollows over their eyes and drooping lower lips, old dim-eyed dogs, old hungry cows like Whitey—the girl felt tender with compassion to think of them. The happy confidence of colts, puppies and calves then seemed a sorrowful thing.

In the darkness the girl felt she would like to take all the sorrows and pains of the animals on her shoulders, as Christ is said to take all the sins and sorrows of mankind unto himself.

She turned over and deliberately controlled her thoughts. Last night I saw a purple cow. I did. The sunset flushed the hillside and old Whitey took on the color. I should love this month. Spring is pretty, but never are colors as fierce and strong as in November. Shade is never so cold and sunshine never so hot. This time everything is intense. That's why I feel so bad sometimes. Or else so very glad.

When she was out with the cattle in the morning she realized that it was because she was so near to earth and animals that the atmosphere of this particular season influenced her thoughts. She didn't feel as comfortable and contented as she had those first days when she took the cows along the road. The intensity of this time of year brightened and darkened her emotions, so every thought had become a keen feeling. If she hated anyone now she would hate fiercely. Equally fierce would be her love.

CHAPTER 46 ⤳

She sat watching the grazing cows and not thinking of anything special when Dirk's uncle came along. Since Dirk
went back east the girl had avoided his people. She was
afraid they might ask her what she had heard from Dirk
lately, and she couldn't say "Nothing at all" without showing how disappointed she felt.

Now Dirk's uncle got out of the car and came walking toward her. She wanted to say, "Why hello there, how
are you?" in a natural sort of way. Instead she watched him
approach as if she were watching a stranger. Could it be
that he had some message for her from Dirk? She could-
n't understand why Dirk should send a message by his
uncle instead of writing to her himself. So she watched and
waited, not knowing what to expect.

Dirk's uncle was frowning. "I've been studying about
something," he said, and the girl held breathlessly still.

"Seems like maybe it might do Dirk good for you to write to him. You know he set an awful lot of store by you."

Surprised, the girl said, "Why, I sort of was waiting. Thought he might write to me first."

"I guess he won't be able to. And I thought, maybe, hearing from you might kind of cheer him up."

"Cheer him up? What do you mean?" She stared at the man and then put out her hand and touched the cloth of his sleeve. "You had better tell me. What happened?"

"Why, child, I thought by now you knew. At first, when it happened, the boy said not to tell you. But now, why, haven't you heard?"

The girl didn't move. Dirk's uncle cleared his throat. "Well, you know there was that accident. And then, they thought it was only temporary because his back was hurt. But it seems that, well—now they aren't sure. He might not be any different. Not ever. And they put a radio by his bed, thought he loved music so and all. But he won't have it. Seems like he can't bear to hear any kind of music."

The girl didn't know if she had said anything or not. She didn't know what she had done. She did remember the misery in the man's face when he went on talking. She saw the misery in his face and the darkness that had fallen everywhere, so that when he went she turned away, and stumbled, and now she lay on the earth, heavy limbed and tired.

Now the only way the earth could be kind was if it would cover her over. She was stretched out on a grave-size piece of earth. And all the earth was a grave, the whole sphere was a grave charging through space, and there were flowers on it, and trees.

There was sunshine, too, warm on her body. A squirrel was scolding endlessly about something, and there was a meadowlark singing. In November.

She thought she had been unhappy because she hadn't known what Dirk felt about her. She had thought she couldn't bear it if Dirk came to love someone else. Or if he died.

Now none of that mattered. If that was all that was wrong she would be happy, whether she knew it or not. She hadn't known the taste of trouble before this. She could laugh at what she had thought was something to worry over.

This was so different. Hopeless was a word, and she had said it lots of times. But now it wasn't a word, it was a feeling, it was an existing reality, it was the whole of everything.

She wanted not to think. But now she kept thinking, and seeing truth sharply, and the sharpness was pain. It was the pain of it that kept her mind so clear, when she wanted it just to be dull with sorrow, as when something dies.

She remembered all that she had been thinking, about death and about the lives of people and animals. She had pondered so much about accepting things. Now she knew that it wasn't a question of accepting anything. She didn't accept tragedy. Tragedy accepted her.

She saw clearly that there was nothing to do. First she thought that she would go to Dirk. Go and find him living wearily, unable to die and unable to move about. His face growing thinner and his eyes not as they had been.

It would be no comfort for him to see her. If he loved her she could bring him only more sorrow.

November Grass

She felt like crying at his uncle's idea. Write him a letter. What would she say? I'm sorry you are paralyzed. The white cow is going to have another calf. We expect it to rain soon....

There was a spider in the grass. She crushed it with her fingers. There was only one way in which man showed more compassion toward animals than toward his own kind. When a horse was hurt too badly to get well it was shot.

His people were so unknowing. If the girl were to be forever resting on a bed she couldn't bear it if horses were running outside her window. Music would torment Dirk as nothing else would.

The little calves sent to the butcher were better off than Dirk. All the pitiful forms of life that came into the world to suffer and die were no worse off. The girl had sorrowed over calves and lambs, felt misery at the sight of a truckload of fat steers.

The calves she had sold must have felt her tenderness toward them.

Dirk must know. One way or the other it would pain him. If he didn't love her at all, it would make him sorry to know how much she cared. If he loved her the pain of it would be almost too great to endure.

The girl didn't know what to do. Now there was no help anywhere. The sun was tender on the hills and the cattle were grazing. Squirrels hurried over the rocks, birds sang, dead leaves kept falling. This beautiful grave that was the earth kept moving toward infinity.

CHAPTER 47 ⁐

Once long ago the girl had said, "I've cried so much over calves and dogs and old horses that have died, I wonder if I will have tears for myself."

Now she had no tears for Dirk. She sat and looked at the cows and Pete and Flaxie that next morning and her eyes felt hard. Tears might soften the heavy thing that pressed against her, something solid as a stone crowding her body.

If I want, she thought, I can climb a hill. Or I can jump on Pete and gallop down the road. But Dirk must stay in one place. Maybe for a year. Maybe forever.

She looked at the familiar things all about—trees, stones, bare fields, and the animals that were her companions. She fingered the ears of the hound, Juno, and Juno looked at her as if she knew how the girl was troubled.

She knew that Dirk loved her. She had started to realize that when she had thought back over his uncle's words.

"At first when it happened the boy said not to tell you....You know he set an awful lot of store by you...."

She thought it a strange thing that she had ever doubted that he loved her. Hadn't he said it over and over again in the expression of his eyes, the tone of his voice?

He might have thought that he was waiting to be sure of himself or of her. He was naturally a person of restraint; she had liked that quality of his. The coming of love, she felt now, should be somehow elusive, should advance and retreat, should be maddening and full of sweet bewilderment. It was the element of wonder that made it so delightful. Love should not be too assured at first.

Remembering, the girl could see how she had been even more secretive than Dirk. So that he must have been doubtful, too. Some instinct had kept her from showing her feeling.

They had been only at the beginning of their adventure. Had nothing happened, Dirk would have written, she would have answered, something would have kept growing until they saw each other again.

She kept thinking, if Dirk had only told me what he felt we could have been happy for a little time.

How dearly beautiful everything should seem to her. When she had longed to know that Dirk loved her she had imagined the ecstasy she might feel. She had thought that everything she saw would be vivid with beauty, would have a meaning for Dirk and her alone.

Now that she knew of Dirk's love everything was so different from the way she had dreamed it that there was bitterness in shadows and sorrow in sunlight.

The false brightness of November was a dreary thing. November grass had no life in it; though the animals grazed everlastingly it would nourish them little. It was nothing but sun-dried withered stuff. The girl felt as if her life was through with growing too.

To think of what might have been was a torment she must stop inflicting on herself.

That is what her mother had said. The girl must make herself grow quiet, wait and see what there is to be done. But what is there to be done, she thought, trying to remember the quiet way her mother had spoken. It was strange how much her mother had known about her all along.

She stretched out and looked up at the quiet sky. Quiet as her mother's eyes. But, she thought, my mother hasn't always been like this. The reason she knows so much about me must be because she felt about my father as I feel about Dirk. She must have wondered if she could care enough to change her whole life around and accept his ways. There must have been times when she wanted to leave him and go back to the things she knew. But she found she belonged wherever my father belonged.

The girl shaded her eyes to watch a gliding eagle, so high over a hill it looked small as a sparrow. If she could be that remote she could see things better, but she felt too near to all the sorrowing earth.

CHAPTER 48 ☙

An east wind came that night. It blew all the way from the desert, over mountains, across valleys. There were many voices in the wind. The girl sat up in bed, but there was nothing she could see. Not even a star. There was destruc tion out there in the night. She could hear the crying of the tormented.

By morning the wind was less fierce. It had shifted so that it was from the southeast. The last dry leaf was taken from the trees, and branches were strewn along the road. There was no sun in the sky. Only cold dark clouds. Yesterday the land had been bright. Now it was desolate, dust lay everywhere.

The cows did not like the gritty grass. They wandered aimlessly, looking for clean forage. There was no bird song and squirrels weren't feeling lively. Everything hated the wind.

Only the old couple who lived up the road faced the wind cheerfully. Mister had called when they went past. He said that the wind would soon be in the south. "South wind brings rain."

"Mister's fixin' to plow soon," his wife said.

The wind sounded despairing, as though it were driven against its will to tear at trees and scatter dust. The girl sat shivering, feeling lost and small. She had spent days in the sunshine thinking. Now her cows and horses were hungry, and what good had all her thinking done? The knowledge of Dirk's love brought her no gladness, only infinite sorrow.

The wind scraped around on the ground as if it, too, was looking for forage. The girl listened to the searching wind. The trees had felt its destruction. She looked at them pityingly. A tree looks maimed where a branch has been torn away.

She tried to remember the hours she had spent with Dirk. All the warm summer days. The gentle nights sweet with the crying of poor-wills and killdeer. She wanted to remember everything he had said, until summer would not seem so long ago, or Dirk so far away.

The wind made it hard to remember summer. The wind has such a lonesome sound, she thought. Lonely as surf beating on an uninhabited shore.

Dirk had loved the sound of surf. He was a listening person; the smallest of sounds had meaning for him. She wondered what strange music he would hear in this wind. The wind was such an old, old thing; it must go forlornly sweeping over the earth. All the winds were one wind, the girl thought. This harsh shifting wind was the same that came softly on summer nights, a sad sort of wind. This was the same wind that brought the winter rains and the smell of spring. Last night it had been a cruel force, but now it was growing tired.

Juno crept close to her and it was as though the old hound and the girl were trying to comfort each other.

If Dirk were here he would be thinking of the wind's wide stretch of desert with its shifting dunes. Some dunes looked like transfixed waves, as if the desert remembered the sea, and Dirk would be thinking that the desert was restless. The wind would speak to him of the weirdly shaped hills at the desert's edge. It would be the song of remote wastes that were beautiful in desolation.

In the wind's voice he would hear the crying of all the earthborn. It would be a sound both sorrowful and triumphant. The wind would not be hateful to him. He would see beyond its destruction.

She began to cry, and her tears were not all sorrow for herself and Dirk. She cried for the strange beauty of the silent things on earth. She cried for its people. For old Mister and Missus, for John of the Wilderness, for her mother and father, for all who must live...

All winds are one wind, she thought, and all lives are one life. She knew why she trembled for hunted deer, why she grieved for calves and felt pity for young foals.

The hound watched her with imploring eyes. "It's all right, Juno," the girl whispered. The trees became wonderfully still and the dark fields waited.

Judy Van der Veer

Once she had listened to music and sorrowed for all the world. Now, as then, her compassion was not for herself. It was not for Dirk. It was over everything, like the heavy clouds that were cold as death and promising as life.

She looked at the sky and the patient fields and the torn trees. There was no shade and no sunshine. Each thing stood apart, before a gray background.

She stood up, facing the wind.

It's surely going to rain, she thought. First the November grass would be cleaned of dust. Then it would be destroyed, rotted and beaten into the drenched earth. It would do good there, too. It would be a kind covering for the pale new grass.

ABOUT THE AUTHOR ☙

Judy Van der Veer (1912–1982) was born in Oil City, Pennsylvania, but spent most of her life in the backcountry of San Diego, on a ranch her father bought near Ramona. Her writing reflects her love of ranch life and her deep appreciation of nature. She wrote a regular column for the *Christian Science Monitor*. Besides *November Grass*, her books include *The River Pasture, A Few Happy Ones, Hold the Rein Free, Higher Than the Arrow,* and two children's books, *Wallace the Wandering Pig* and *To the Rescue*.